RED ENERGY
(Cold Energy part 2)
The Alex Cave Series book 3.

Written by James M. Corkill.

The characters and events in this book are fictitious. Any similarity to real persons, living or dead is coincidental and not intended by the author.

ALASKA. A TINY ISLAND IN THE ALEUTIAN CHAIN:

Geophysics instructor Alex Cave entered the opening in the rock face of the volcano and saw the light from his flashlight reflecting off a mirror surface. He followed the mirror deeper into the volcano until he reached the airlock doors of the alien spacecraft and stepped into a large, circular room. His light reflected off a six-foot diameter sphere with a mirror surface before he aimed the flashlight at the floor, exposing the powdered remains of a human-shaped body in a one-piece silver suit. As he picked up the shiny fabric, the powder flowed through the material onto the floor. "Tough luck for the first time traveler."

He set it aside while removing all his clothes and stepped into the suit. "I hope this works." He cautiously placed his palms against the mirror surface of the sphere, felt an electrical shock, and vanished.

***

FIVE DAYS EARLIER.
THE MYSTIC:

On the bridge, Mike wasn't paying much attention to Alex talking on the phone when he heard the deep thumping of an approaching helicopter. He grabbed the binoculars and looked toward the sound, and when he focused the lenses, he smiled and looked over at Alex, who ended his call. "The Coast Guard helicopter is coming our way."

Alex took the binoculars from Mike and focused on the orange and white helicopter half a mile from the island. At least he had some support, although they probably wouldn't have much firepower. Still, it was better than no support at all until the military arrived.

His smile turned into a frown as he recognized a trail of white smoke streaking through the sky and he stood up. The helicopter was suddenly a massive ball of fire, with flaming pieces dropping into the ocean.

Mike jumped out of his chair and stared at the smoke over the water. "What just happened?"

Alex aimed the binoculars toward origin of the trail of smoke and saw two large helicopters headed toward them. "We're being invaded." He grabbed the microphone for the portable radios. "Are you listening, Rita?"

"I heard an explosion. What just happened?"

"Two helicopters just shot down a Coast Guard rescue helicopter, and they're coming our way."

"What do you want me to do?"

"Tell Henry and David to stay inside the spaceship until we know what's going on. I'll be there in a minute, so meet me on the dock." He looked at Mike. "I'll grab the shotguns and take the motorboat to the island while you get the Mystic away from here."

"That's a bad plan, Alex. I can help."

"Thanks, but the Mystic's too vulnerable."

Alex grabbed the binoculars and stared out the window for one last look at the approaching helicopters. "You can come back when they leave."

"And do what? Collect the bodies?"

"I hope not."

***

Rita shoved the radio into the chest pocket of her coat and placed her hand on the butt of the pistol inside her coat pocket. She knew in a few minutes, all hell was going to break loose, so she stepped inside the spaceship.

David heard the explosion and was moving toward the exit when Rita stepped in his way. "What's going on?"

"We're going to have company in a few minutes. Just stay inside, and I'll go find out what happened."

Rita hurried back to the dock and could see Alex standing in the motorboat at the stern of the *Mystic*, collecting shotguns from Mike and placing them on one of the seats. She waited while Alex drove across to the island, keeping her pistol hidden in her pocket.

Alex eased the motorboat against the dock. "One helicopter is a troop carrier, and the other one is for cargo. I brought shotguns for you and David."

He reached down and grabbed one shotgun, then handed it to Rita. As he reached down for the other two, he heard the distinct sound of the pump handle inserting a round into the chamber of a shotgun. When he looked up, Rita was aiming it at his chest. "What are you doing?"

"Throw the shotguns into the water."

Alex stared at her. "We're in a lot of trouble, so don't do this." He eased his hand down to his jean pocket.

Rita brought her shotgun up to her shoulder and sighted down the barrel at Alex. "Don't even think about it! I know about your pistol. Take it out slowly and toss it into the water."

Alex knew he didn't stand a chance and held her gaze and did as she asked. "Why are you doing this?"

"Get rid of the shotguns."

Alex reached down, grabbed the barrel of a shotgun, and then looked at Rita. He thought about using it as a club, but she shook her head no, so he tossed both of them into the water. "What now?"

"Go back to the Mystic and take it away from the island." She saw the rage building in Alex's eyes. "I don't want to see the Mystic full of holes, so just do what I say and no one will get hurt."

Alex moved forward to the steering wheel, but hesitated to sit down. "What do you want?"

Rita brought the shotgun down even with her waist, but kept the barrel aimed at Alex. "We want the devices."

"Who are you working for?"

"Not working *for,* Alex. Working *with,* and you don't need to know. Just leave and I won't hurt anyone."

"Right, like your friends didn't hurt anyone in the Coast Guard helicopter a few minutes ago?"

"I had nothing to do with that. Now leave!"

Alex reluctantly drove the motorboat away from the dock, while the deep thumping of the approaching helicopters was getting louder. He knew if they didn't leave the area right away, the invaders might capture the *Mystic.* If that happened, he could not come back and get his friends. He didn't trust Rita to keep her word, and his friends might be dead when he returned, but he knew he had no choice.

When he reached the stern of the *Mystic,* he tied the motorboat off to a cleat and ran up the stairs onto the bridge. He didn't answer the question in Mike's eyes. He switched the engines from thrusters to jet pumps, then shoved the throttle to full speed and steered away from the island.

***

Rita waited on the dock until the *Mystic* was racing away, then headed back toward the spaceship. If everything went according to plan, in a few months she would be wealthy enough to buy a small island.

***

David stood in the entrance of the alien craft, watching Rita walking up the beach. "Where's Alex?"

Rita stopped just outside the spaceship. "He'll come back once the helicopters leave. Get back inside."

David hesitated to do as she asked. "I don't understand. What's going on?"

"We're taking the device in the cave. Just do what I say, and no one will get hurt." When David didn't move, she aimed the shotgun at him, but he just glared back. "I'm not kidding."

David slowly turned and went back inside, and saw the questioning expression from Henry. "Alex isn't coming. They want one of the devices, so just stay calm, and maybe we can find a way out of this."

David got an idea and slowly walked to the four chairs in the center of the control room. He saw Rita watching him through the opening as he sat down and waited for her reaction, but she didn't pay him any attention. He knew if he could shut down the power and seal them inside this ship, they would be safe from whoever was coming. He figured if the exterior of this alien craft could survive in molten rock for one-hundred and eighty-million years, a shotgun blast would not hurt it.

Rita turned and looked up as a helicopter suddenly appeared over the edge of the crater, then four thick nylon ropes dropped out of the open side door. An instant later, four armed men slid down them to the beach.

Rita saw David reaching down to the control pad and stepped inside, holding the shotgun waist high, and aimed it at David. "Come over here, Henry. We're going outside."

Henry's mouth opened slightly as he looked at David for help. David lowered his hand toward the control panel to cut the power before Henry made it to the exit, but flinched and jerked his hands away when the deafening roar from the shotgun's warning blast filled the room.

David stared at Rita as she swung the shotgun around from the exit and aimed it at him, then raised his hands. "All right! You've made your point." He saw the imploring look in Henry's eyes. "I'm sorry, Doc."

Henry's shoulders sagged as he slowly shuffled across the room and out through the entrance. "What do you want, Rita?"

"Just stand over there away from the ship until we're done."

***

Using a pair of binoculars, Alex stared back at the two helicopters hovering over the island, frustrated there was nothing he could do. He watched as four men dropped down ropes from the first helicopter and disappeared into the crater, and then the aircraft moved off to one side of the island to allow the second aircraft, a Sikorsky S-94 cargo helicopter, to move into position. Two thick cables with slings quickly descended, and a few moments later, the device from the entrance of the cave was hoisted into the air, swaying below the helicopter as it moved away.

The first aircraft returned and hovered over the crater, and Alex watched as two people in harnesses on the end of a rope were pulled into the helicopter. For an instant, he thought one of them had gray hair. Four more people were hoisted out of the crater, and he recognized a full head of red hair. "Damn you Rita!"

He watched as the last four people disappeared inside the aircraft and both helicopters swung away from the island. "Take us back, Mike."

Mike brought the *Mystic* close to the island and set the controls on autopilot, and then he and Alex ran out from the bridge and hurried down the stairs to the motorboat, still tied to the stern.

When Alex looked across at the island, he saw David walking down to the dock, and sighed with relief he wasn't dead. He jumped into the boat, and motored over to the island. As the boat bumped against the dock, he noticed David's angry expression. "Get in. We'll wait on the *Mystic* until help arrives."

"That bitch Rita took the Doc, Alex."

"I know. Now get in so we can figure out where she took him."

Alex took them back to the *Mystic*, where Mike was waiting on the stern. They all walked up the outside stairs to the bridge, and no one spoke for several long moments until David broke the silence. "At least we have the location of the other three devices."

Alex gave him a somber look. "I'm more worried about what Rita has planned for the device she did get. They may have been designed to clean the atmosphere, but we know how potentially destructive they can be as well. Once we get some support out here, I'm going back to the mainland. The only way to find the Doc is to find out whom Rita is working with, and if he comes to any harm, she'll wish she had never met me."

David had seen that look in Alex's eyes once before, when he had talked about the six men who had murdered his wife, Sevi. Alex had killed each one without mercy.

Chapter 1

WYOMING:

When Henry felt a thud from the tire, he opened his eyes and looked at one of two guards sitting in the back of the cargo truck with him. The guard sitting beside him had his head tilted back against the wall, snoring softly. He was glad they had respected his age, or perhaps Rita had told them to be considerate, but they had not even tied his hands.

He hadn't seen Rita since the helicopters had landed at a private airport in Yakama, Washington, and had no idea where they were taking him. He looked down at the device strapped onto a wooden pallet, wondering what had made her do this. She appeared to enjoy working for Mike on the research ship, so was it for money?

He felt the truck slow down as it turned a corner and stopped, and then he heard men talking outside, but the conversations were muffled. When the truck began moving again, the road felt rough, tossing him from side to side. When it stopped again, one of the guards stood and opened the rear door, allowing the dwindling sunlight to illuminate the interior.

Rita looked at Henry sitting on the bench seat against the far wall. "Sorry for the rough treatment, but there was only enough room in the cab for two."

Henry remained seated. "I will not help you, Rita."

"Fine. I'll take you somewhere for dinner. I even have a place for you to sleep."

Henry felt his stomach rumble when he thought about food, and then slowly stood and moved past the device to the rear of the truck. When Rita reached out to help him down, he shrugged her off and climbed out on his own. "I could use something to eat, but I will not change my mind."

Rita knew Henry was tired and didn't push the issue. "That's okay. I'll explain everything in the morning. Follow me."

When Henry walked around the truck, he froze and stared at Rita. "Are we going underground?"

"That's right. It's an old research facility."

Henry felt his heart rate increase. "I do not do well underground."

"I promise you, it's safe."

Henry turned and stared at the entrance into the facility. It was an arched shaped concrete opening, twenty feet high and fifteen feet across at the bottom, similar to a tunnel entrance on a highway. The letters C.O.B.R.A. were imbedded in the concrete above the opening. "What is COBRA?"

"It stands for Complex Organisms and Biological Research, Alien." She indicated a waiting golf cart. "Get in. It's a long walk to the facility."

Henry hesitated. He was not claustrophobic, but was afraid of being buried alive. As a young boy in Germany after World War II, he had been trapped for three days in a flimsy old bomb shelter, hastily constructed during a raid, and he was not eager to be below ground again.

A big man put his hand on Henry's shoulder. "I'll make sure you're safe, Doctor Heinz."

Henry turned and looked up at a different guard. "Forgive me, but I do not even know your name, sir."

"Chris Jenkins and I'll be your escort while you're here, Doctor. I'll do my best to make you as comfortable as possible."

Henry turned and reluctantly climbed into the rear seat. Once Rita sat in the front, Chris climbed in behind the steering wheel and drove into the entrance. Fluorescent lights flashed by overhead illuminating the concrete floor and walls curving up to form the arched ceiling and Henry felt a knot form in his stomach.

Three-hundred-yards further, the tunnel ended at a fifty-foot-square, steel-framed opening. On the left side, massive hinges supported a two-foot thick steel door for sealing the facility, which only added to Henry's anxiety.

They drove through the opening into an enormous circular chamber three hundred feet across at the bottom, with a ceiling shaped like a dome, fifty feet high. Thick steel rods hung from the ceiling, supporting a grid-work of metal rails with several mechanical hoists.

Chris stopped the golf cart just inside the entrance and the three of them climbed out, and then he led them into the lounge and indicated the table and chairs. "Why don't you two take a seat and I'll fix us something to eat."

After they sat down, Henry stared at Rita. "Will you at least tell me why you brought the device to this facility?"

"We need a safe place to conduct our experiments. This facility is leased from the government by the D.A.R Corporation. DAR is short for Demolition and Reconstruction. They get contracts with the government and local municipalities after any major disaster, such as hurricanes, tornadoes, bombings, and just about every major catastrophe here in the states. It's a billion dollar industry for those who get the contracts."

"I do not understand. Why do you need the device?"

Rita knew why, but also knew if she told Henry, it would only strengthen his resolve not to cooperate. "All in good time."

Henry thought about the heavy steel door. "Did you see the movie, The Andromeda Strain?"

Rita grinned. "Both versions, and you're right to make the association. During the beginning of the space program in the sixties, the government was worried about bringing samples back from the moon. They set up this abandoned gold mine as a place to study the material, and in 1970, the facility was sealed. One day, a congressional representative convinced the government this place was outdated and a wasted resource and should be leased under contract to the highest bidder. The owner of DAR, Steve Preston, underbid his competitors, and now has full use of this facility."

Henry found it odd this complex would be sealed and abandoned without a reason. He was about to bring it to Rita's attention when Chris walked out of the kitchen and set a platter of sliced club sandwiches on the table.

"It's the best I could do on short notice. I'm actually a pretty good cook."

The conversations ceased while they ate. When they finished, Chris took the platter back to the kitchen and returned to the table, but did not sit down. "I'm sure you're as tired as I am, Doctor. Let me show you to your room and where the restrooms are located. You'll find an assortment of blue coveralls in the dresser if you want to change into something clean."

Henry slid his chair back and stood, as did Rita, before they followed Chris to the back of the lounge through another door. After showing them the washrooms, he led them into the small dormitory style sleeping quarters.

***

When Henry awoke the next morning, he searched through the drawers and found the smallest coverall he could find, and then carried it down the hall to the showers. When he returned to the lounge, he saw Chris sitting at a table.

Chris looked up from his magazine and grinned when Henry entered the room. The coverall he was wearing hung loosely over his small frame, and the pant legs were rolled up above his shoes. "Good morning, Doctor Heinz. Would you like something to eat?"

Henry continued across the room and sat at the table. "Yes, thank you. Toast and coffee would be nice."

Chris stood. "I'll try to get you a smaller size coverall while you're eating."

Henry stared after Chris as he walked around the counter. For being so robust in build, around two-hundred and fifty pounds and perhaps six foot tall, Chris carried the weight well. When he returned with the toast and coffee, Henry noticed Chris's nose had been broken at one time and never properly reset, and a slight scar ran through his right eyebrow. When Chris set the plate of toast on the table, Henry saw the scars on his knuckles.

Chris notice Henry staring at his hand and moved it away. "I'll go look for some different coveralls that might fit you better, Doctor Heinz."

Despite being held captive, Henry appreciated Chris's courteous attitude. "Just Henry will do, Chris. Thank you."

When Chris left the lounge, Henry slid the magazine over and read the title. Better Homes and Gardens was not what he had expected.

A few moments later, Chris returned clutching a pair of light blue coveralls and set them on the table. "These are the smallest size I could find, but they should fit you better than the ones you have on. Mister Preston just arrived, and he's eager to meet you." Chris noticed the magazine was face up and grinned. "I enjoy gardening in my spare time."

Henry found Chris to be a curious individual. Perhaps he was just a man with a job to do, and did not bear him any ill will. When he realized Chris was waiting for him to change clothes, he got up and hurried back to the bunk room.

***

After parking the golf cart at the entrance, Rita ran over to the helicopter as Steve Preston climbed out. It had been two months since she had left him to work for Mike Tanner on the *Mystic*. She threw her arms around his neck, pulling him close for a passionate kiss. "I've missed you so much."

Preston stared at the entrance, not Rita. "Missed you, too. Take me inside. I want to see what this alien device looks like."

***

When Henry walked in, Chris set the magazine down and stood from the table. "Much better."

Henry followed him into the massive main chamber and saw the device positioned vertically on a support base with the pointed end up. A framework of one-inch fiberglass rods held it in place.

He looked across the room and was relieved to see the heavy steel door was still open, and then saw Rita standing in front of an elevated control console. Apparently, Rita had brought a suitcase and was dressed in blue jeans and a light blue sweater, and beside her was a handsome man dressed in a white shirt and black jeans.

Rita looked up when Henry and Chris entered the room. "Come over here and join us."

Henry strolled beside Chris to the console, where Preston held his hand out to him, but Henry refused to accept it. "I do not appreciate being kidnapped, Sir." When the man's eyes showed his hostility, Henry raised his chin defiantly and returned his stare.

"I don't give a shit. Teach us how to control this device and you'll be treated decently. Refuse and I'll strip you naked and put you on display to the outside world. There are thousands of sick people on the internet who would enjoy seeing you humiliated."

Since he had always been very modest, Henry's jaw dropped slightly when he realized the man was serious. He closed his mouth and gave Preston a nod of acceptance.

Chris's right hand unconsciously made a fist when he heard Preston's threat and placed a reassuring left hand on Henry's shoulder. "Just do as he asks and everything will be okay. I promise."

When Henry looked up, he saw the sincerity in Chris's eyes. "Thank you, but I will only do what is necessary."

Preston turned to Rita. "Do you really need this old man's help?"

"He knows more about this device than I do."

Preston glared at Henry. "Fine. Just let me know when he's no longer of any use and I'll get rid of him." When he saw the fear in Henry's eyes, he grinned sadistically. "Glad to see you'll give us your full cooperation, Doctor."

Rita shifted her stance when Henry stared at her, his eyes begging for help, and then she looked at Preston. "I'm sure he won't be a problem."

Preston gave her a quick kiss. "I'd better get going. Chris? Drive me back to the helicopter."

Once Chris and Preston drove down the tunnel, Henry stared at Rita. "I do not know as much as you think I do. You have seen how unpredictable the devices can be, and the repercussions of your experiments could have devastating effects. Please stop this before it is too late."

"Sorry, Henry. I think you know more than you're telling me. Just help me get it right and nothing bad will happen."

Henry sighed in frustration and headed for the lounge. "You will be the death of us all, Miss Harrow."

Chapter 2

COBRA ONE WEEK LATER:

Henry sat hunched over at the table, poking at his scrambled eggs with a fork. He had worked for the government doing secret research for over fifty years, so he knew there must have been a very important reason COBRA had been shut down in 1970. The fact it had also been sealed only added to his concern, so he looked across the table at Chris. "Do you know what they did in this facility?"

"Nope. Rita might know."

"I have already asked her, and she does not."

Chris smirked at him. "Would you like to see the actual COBRA laboratory?"

Henry sat up straight. "Yes. Perhaps if I could see what type of equipment they were using, it would give me a better understanding of why they sealed the entrance."

They stood, and Henry followed Chris out of the lounge and across the main room to the elevator. He looked across at Rita, who didn't look up from the control console. He had not been much help, and Rita had a better understanding of resonate frequencies than he did. He was just grateful she had not told Preston he was useless.

The elevator door opened, and when they stepped inside the cab, Henry noticed all four numbers on the control panel pointed down. As the floor seemed to drop beneath his feet, he tried to control his growing anxiety. When the door opened on the third floor, he released a deep sigh of relief.

They stepped out and the overhead fluorescent lighting came on automatically. The laboratory was a single large room with several workstations, and Henry strolled around the tables, trying to picture in his mind what they were doing down here.

Old, dust covered test equipment had been abandoned on the tables, along with several containment chambers with rubber gloves poking inside. Against one wall, empty cages were stacked three high, but when he stepped closer, he recognized the skeletal remains of monkeys inside them and turned back to Chris. "This is not a good sign. I can tell you this much. Whatever the reason, they left in a hurry."

"What makes you say that?"

"Those animals were abandoned in the cages, which mean something must have quickly gone wrong with their experiments on the moon samples. If I could contact my associates, we may learn exactly what happened here."

Chris stared at Henry for a long moment. Now, he too was concerned, but he didn't want to lose his job. "I wish I could help you, Henry. I really do. But I have responsibilities."

"I understand, Chris. We cannot always control our lives."

Chris glanced at the elevator door. "We're not supposed to be down here, so we should go back to the test area before Rita notices we're gone."

"She knows we are down here. I think she does not care as long as I cannot contact the outside world."

"Do you want to stay here for a while longer?"

Henry looked around one last time. "No. There is nothing more to learn down here."

Henry stepped into the elevator and noticed there was still one more floor below this one. Apparently, it could only be accessed by a key in the control panel. As the doors closed and the cab rose, his phobia slowly subsided. When the door opened and he stepped out of the elevator on the main floor, his phobia` stopped.

Rita was still standing over the control console, and Henry wasn't sure if either she didn't notice their arrival, or didn't care as they continued across the room. Henry stopped next to the device and had a deep sense of apprehension about this test, but knew to argue the point again would be useless.

Rita looked up at her companions. "You're just in time. I'm ready to try the first combination of resonate frequencies. You two might want to move away from the device."

Henry continued across the room and saw the excitement in Rita's eyes as she held her finger over the activation button.

She grinned down at Henry. "Are you ready?"

"Do not do this, Rita."

She turned back to watch the device. "Here we go. Three, two, one, now."

Henry held his breath as the seconds on the digital clock clicked past three, four, five, and six, but nothing happened. He released a long sigh of relief when the device remained inactive, but then the concrete floor sent a vibration into the soles of their shoes. It only lasted for a fraction of a second and they did not see any change to the device.

"What just happened?" Chris asked.

Rita studied the information on the digital display. "Nothing happened. The test is a bust. We'll need to try again with a different combination of frequencies."

Henry shook his fist as he glared at Rita. "You are wrong! You felt the movement in the floor. Something happened, but it was not what you expected. We have no idea why this facility was sealed, so you must not proceed with your experiments!"

Chris was momentarily stunned by the fury in Henry's argument, and suddenly he felt afraid of the device. For a moment, he wondered if losing his job might be a better option.

When Rita turned back to the console, Henry let his shoulders slump. "I can help you, Rita. I could contact

Director Donner and have the records of this COBRA project sent by courier."

Rita gave him a stern look. "Absolutely not. No one can know our location until I determine it's necessary. I'll use *my* contacts to find out what happened here. Is that clear?"

Henry lowered his head in defeat, knowing something terrible will result from her impatience. He shuffled toward the lounge as his only refuge.

Chris noticed Henry's depression and decided a walk outside might help him. "Listen, Henry. Mister Preston should arrive shortly. I'll need to pick him up at the entrance anyway, so let's go for a ride outside."

Henry followed Chris over to the golf cart and climbed into the passenger seat. Once Chris was in, they rode along the tunnel in silence.

***

Chris parked just inside the entrance, and they climbed out and strolled outside. Henry stopped to look around. It had been dusk when he had arrived, but now he was seeing it in full daylight, and it appeared to be a state park. There were no vehicles on the half-moon shaped area, which ended one hundred feet away at a forest of thick-trunked evergreens.

He slid his shoe across what appeared to be dirt, but was actually a hard surface covered with tan-colored epoxy paint. Blotches of charcoal gray and green paint were scattered randomly in every direction to complete a camouflaged tapestry. His depression deepened when he realized from the air, it would appear to be a clearing in the forest, and no one would suspect he would be there.

Chris indicated a clear area under the branches. "There's a bench over there if you want to sit for a while."

Henry went over and sat down, and stared down at the pine needles on the ground as he stirred them with the toe of his shoe. Without realizing it, he had drawn the capitals A and C. He looked over at Chris. "Do you know what their intentions are if they can control the device?"

"No. I'm just one of the guards and do what they say."

"There are more guards at this facility?"

"Yeah, but they just take care of the entry gate and patrol the grounds. I live in there and take care of the internal security, but usually there isn't much for me to do. I needed something to occupy my time, so I started taking cooking lessons online."

Henry felt a glimmer of hope he might get a message to Donner over the internet. First, he needed to gather more information about the security at this facility. "How many guards do they have here?"

Chris stared at Henry for a moment. "I hope you're not planning an escape. I like you, Henry, but I can't allow you to leave. I have a job to do. Besides, this place is shaped like a horseshoe, and the surrounding rock is over three hundred feet high and nearly vertical. There is no way to hike up to the rim. The only way out is through the narrow entrance where the guards are stationed, or by helicopter."

As if on cue, Chris heard the deep thumping sound of an approaching helicopter echo off the face of the entrance. "I'm sure that's Mister Preston and we'll get blown away by the downdraft. We need to go back inside."

Henry and Chris hurried across into the entrance and waited while a dull gray, two-person helicopter swooped in low above the treetops and set down on the painted surface. Once the rotors slowed down, Chris walked out to greet Preston, but Henry refused to be friendly and stayed inside.

Preston climbed out of the helicopter and walked with Chris to the entrance. "I heard about the tremor. Is Rita making any headway?"

"Kind of, I guess. She'll have to tell you about it."

Preston grinned sadistically when he saw Henry. "Feeling any better, old man?"

"I would feel better if you told me what you intend to do with that device."

Preston was impressed by the old man's tenacity. "All right. I plan to create a series of storms along the east coast, but nothing too dramatic. I'll have my men and equipment staged nearby, and I can underbid my competitors for the cleanup contract. I'll make millions of dollars in a matter of months."

Henry stared at Preston for a long moment. "You are a madman. You cannot control the weather!"

"I can if you and Rita figure out the correct set of frequencies. I'm going to use them no matter what, so it's up to you and Rita to get it right. If the devices don't work as advertised, they could do more damage than I intend, and it will be your fault, old man."

"What about all the people whose lives you will affect because of the destruction? Possibly their deaths, as well?"

"It happens all the time anyway, so why not take advantage of knowing when and where?"

"This will be different. *You* will be the cause, not a natural event. No. It will be your fault, not mine."

"Then you had better get it right if you want to minimize the damage." He turned to Chris. "Take me inside. I want to talk to Rita about the tremor."

Henry climbed into the rear seat while Preston sat up front next to Chris. Once the cart was driving down the tunnel, Henry leaned forward. "Tell me, Mister Preston. Do you know why this facility was sealed in 1970?"

Preston turned his head to look at Henry. "Not exactly. I heard a rumor the funding was cut off because of an accident. This used to be a mine, so it wouldn't surprise me if they had a cave-in. They probably decided it wasn't worth the cost to reinforce the entire facility."

Henry leaned back, knowing that could not be the reason. It was too simple, and that massive door kept something sealed inside, not outside.

When Chris parked near the entrance to the main room, they climbed out and strolled across to Rita, who turned around and leaned back against the console as she watched their approach. Preston continued until he was face to face with her, and then gently cupped his hand under her chin to draw her lips to his.

When they parted, Rita smiled and released a deep sigh of pleasure. She looked into his soft brown eyes before wrapping her arms around his neck and pulling his body close to hers. "I've missed you," she whispered in his ear.

Preston looked over Rita's shoulder at the device. "Did you figure out how to control that piece of alien technology?"

Rita let go of Preston. "I know why I'm having so much difficulty getting it to work. In order to create the vortex needed to induce a change in weather patterns, we need at least two devices to interact."

"We have the one recovered from the Bering Sea. I can have it brought here, if you like."

"I don't know if it will do us any good. The power supply in that one is nearly depleted." She looked at Henry. "They must use the same crystals as the spaceship. Wouldn't you agree, Doctor?"

Henry crossed his arms. "I do not know. This is the first device I have seen."

Rita knew he was right. "I'll need to open one up to find out for sure, but I would rather use the depleted one, in case something goes wrong on my first attempt."

"I'll set it up. What about the tremor? Do you think it's safe to stay here?"

"I'm sure it's nothing to worry about. We're only one hundred and eighty miles from Yellowstone National Park, and they have earthquakes all the time. That's probably what we felt here."

Preston grinned. "Great. How about a demonstration? You said it almost worked the last time. Show me what it does."

"All right. Watch this."

Henry wanted to protest, but knew it would be pointless. He could only stand by and see what would happen.

When Rita pressed the button, the device shimmered, and a small whirlwind formed above the tip. Everything electronic stopped working until the whirlwind ceased spinning, then a low-pitched rumble echoed around the room as the floor shuddered for an instant before everything was quiet and still.

Preston stared at Rita. "What the hell was that? Did you do it?"

"No. I don't know why that happened."

Preston put his hands on his hips as the devil's grin spread across his face. "I could make a lot of money cleaning up after just one earthquake. You must have caused it, so try it again."

Henry stepped in front of Preston and glared up at him. "Are you insane? Do you not realize that we are underground? This entire facility could collapse on us!"

"Okay, I get your point. We'll take it outside next time." He looked at Rita. "If you can make this device create an earthquake whenever you want to, I'll double the money I promised you."

"It can't be the device, Steve. It's above ground, and that earthquake came from deep beneath us. It was probably just another earthquake at Yellowstone."

"I don't think so. It happen both times you turned on the device."

"That's why I shouldn't try it again until I know for sure."

"All right. I'll have the other device brought to this location." He turned to Chris. "Take me back to the helicopter."

Rita stared after Preston as he walked away without kissing her goodbye. Something had changed since she had left on the Mystic two months ago, and she thought it might be another woman. That's the only explanation for him being so cold to her.

Henry waited until Chris drove Preston out of the facility before giving Rita a pleading expression. "It is not a coincidence, Rita. These seismic events happen when you activate that device, so there must be something in this facility reacting to those specific frequencies." He waited for a reply, but Rita just stared at him. "They sealed this facility for a reason! Please let me call Donner and find out why?"

Rita knew it wasn't a coincidence, but also knew Donner would order Special Forces to storm this facility the moment he found out. She would be arrested for kidnapping if not shot. "I can't let you call him, Henry. I'll wait until I get another device before I try it again. That's all I can do for now."

When Henry shuffled across the room toward the lounge, Rita leaned back on the console. She chewed on her lower lip and crossed her arms, wondering what they were doing here. She had received no information about this facility from her contacts, so perhaps Henry is right. This is the wrong place to conduct the experiment.

Chapter 3

YELLOWSTONE NATIONAL PARK:

Cynthia Barlow was sitting on a wooden bench in front of the Old Faithful Geyser, with her eight-year-old daughter, Sissy. They were waiting for the next scheduled eruption, which was supposed to happen fifteen minutes ago.

Sissy looked at her Mickey Mouse wristwatch, and then up at her mom. "Did somebody forget to turn it on today?"

Cynthia smiled. "That's not how it works. It's an act of nature."

"Then how come it's so late?"

Cynthia looked up when the mixed conversations from the crowd suddenly ceased. "It's starting right now."

When Sissy looked at the geyser, small columns of water sporadically soared ten feet into the air and then crashed down on the calcium-covered rock. "I don't see why this is so interesting."

"Just keep watching. It gets bigger in a few moments."

The next eruption of steaming water soared eighty feet into the air before crashing on to the concrete only one-hundred and fifty-feet in front of Sissy, who flinched. "Is it supposed to do that?"

"Yes, it is. That's why the benches are way over here."

"It was a little scary, but I wouldn't come all the way here just to see it."

Cynthia felt the bench shake as a deep rumble filled the air. The geyser roared out of the ground, climbing higher and higher, as if it would never stop. Screaming voices erupted from the crowd as scalding water crashed down onto the startled spectators. Everyone ran for shelter, pushing and shoving each other out of the way, desperately attempting to escape the steaming deluge.

Cynthia grabbed Sissy's hand, yanking her off the bench as she jumped up and ran toward the hotel and forced her way through the crowd of panicked people into the lobby. When she reached the fireplace in the center of the room, she dropped to her knees and held Sissy at arm's length, "Are you hurt? Did you get burnt?"

"I'm okay, Mommy. What happened? Why did it do that?"

"I don't know, darling. It wasn't supposed to."

Screams echoed in the massive room as injured people shoved their way into the lobby. Cynthia wrapped her arms around Sissy, clutching her tightly against her chest as she stood and moved to one side of the room. She felt Sissy's tears slipping down the side of her neck, and then her own vision blurred with tears, watching parents trying to comfort their wailing children.

***

Myra Epson, the Director of the lodging in the park, was not prepared for the number of burn victims staggering into the Old Faithful Hotel. The ambulance service in the park was limited, and the overwhelmed medical staff consisted of one doctor and four nurses. She had called a small town outside the park for assistance, but they would not arrive for another thirty minutes. Thankfully, the geyser had stopped a few moments after the colossal eruption.

She watched the hotel employees carrying tubs of ice and stacks of white cotton towels into the reception area. As she listened to the screams of the injured children, she fought hard to maintain a calm composure, but her sense of helplessness to ease their suffering threatened to shatter her false facade.

***

When the USGS Representative, Jerry Mercer, arrived at the hotel from the Mammoth Station, he walked across the lobby through remaining injured to Myra, who had been the Director of the park hotels for twelve years. She looked overwhelmed by the sight in the lobby, and he, too, was struggling to keep his emotions in check. "Is there anything I can do to help?"

Myra wiped the tears from her cheeks. "Why did this happen, Jerry?"

"We didn't notice any unusual seismic events in the park, but we're also checking the outlying areas for unusual activity. For the moment, we don't know what caused the geyser to erupt like that."

"We're not set up to handle this type of incident. I just hope Old Faithful doesn't erupt again."

"I saw the maintenance crew outside roping off the area around the geyser, so if it happens again, no one will get hurt. Everything else is far enough away. I'll keep you informed on what we discover."

"Thanks, Jerry."

***

YELLOWSTONE SEISMIC INFORMATION CENTER. MAMMOTH STATION:

Jerry walked into the building and saw his two fellow geophysics experts, Paul Sterling, and Vivian Warner, studying the data on the computers. Technically, he was their supervisor, but they were more like a family. "Have either of you had any luck finding the reason for the event at Old Faithful?"

Vivian shook her head no. "Nothing about it makes any sense."

Paul stood and indicated the large wall-mounted video screen, showing the twelve GPS stations in the park. "The only unit indicating any movement is the one amber light flashing at the Old Faithful station. The elevation under the entire area increased by five inches, but once the event was over, it returned to its previous elevation. It's like the ground under the geyser burped."

Jerry studied the screen. "It's not that I doubt you, Paul, but are you sure the unit is functioning correctly? I mean, that's not possible."

"I'm positive it actually occurred."

"I agree with Paul's findings," said Vivian. "This could be very bad. It means something is happening deep in the caldera."

Jerry turned to Paul. "When is our next opportunity for an INSAR image?" (Interferometric Synthetic Aperture Radar.)

"We won't have access to the satellite for another two weeks. What the heck is going on?"

Jerry stared at the screen. "I have no idea."

Paul frowned. "We're supposed to be the experts, but right now, I feel like a freshman geology student."

The mention of students caused Jerry to think about Alex Cave. He seemed to have an uncanny ability to discover the cause of unusual seismic events. "I have a friend who might help us. Let's just hope that's the end of it."

***

MONTANA STATE COLLEGE, BOZEMAN:

The last senior geophysics student stopped at his desk, and Alex knew what she wanted. Laura was older than his other students were, and had made her intentions clear since the first semester.

Laura smiled at Alex as she slowly used her hand to drape her long hair over one shoulder. "It's Friday, Alex. Will you join me for a drink?"

He found her attractive and outgoing, but when he was close to her, there was no connection. After their third date, he realized he was not over the loss of his wife, even though deep down he knew he should be. "I was just leaving for Wyoming."

"All right. I'll take a rain check. Have a good trip."

"Thanks."

When she smiled and left the room, Alex locked his desk drawers. Since he had arrived home from Alaska nearly a week ago, he had been anxiously awaiting information about Henry, but so far, not even Director Donner had found him. He was still baffled by the sphere in the cargo hold of the spacecraft. Did it function as part of the ship? Did it have some sort of electrical charge? He found not knowing frustrating.

His phone rang, and the caller ID was his friend in Yellowstone National Park. "Hey, Jerry."

"I hope I'm not interrupting your class, Professor."

Alex grinned when he heard Jerry's baritone voice, since he was only five-foot tall. "I was just on my way out. What's going on?"

"We're getting some strange activity in the Yellowstone caldera. We're not sure what to make of it, and I could use your expertise. Any chance you could come to my office at the Mammoth Station?"

Alex hesitated to reply. Okawna had asked him to come to his hometown for his father's funeral tomorrow afternoon, and a detour through the park would add two hours to his four-hour drive this evening. "There's someplace I need to be tomorrow, and I was just getting ready to leave. Can it wait until I get back?"

Jerry explained what had happened with Old Faithful earlier today. "We can't figure out the cause, Alex. I could really use your help."

Alex knew the Yellowstone Super Volcano erupts about every seven-hundred and fifty-thousand years, and was already past due for another major eruption, and he wondered if the incident might be a sign it was becoming active again. "I'll detour through the park on my way and be there in an hour."

"That would be great, Alex. I'll be waiting."

Alex slipped the phone into his coat pocket, grabbed his briefcase, and locked the door behind him on his way to the parking lot. His suitcase was already sitting on the back seat, so he climbed into his SUV and drove south toward Yellowstone.

***

YELLOWSTONE NATIONAL PARK. MAMMOTH STATION:

When Jerry saw Alex walk through the doorway, he stood from behind his desk and hurried around to greet him. "Glad you could make it."

Alex reached down to shake the little man's hand. "You got my attention when you said you don't know what's happening. You're the guru of this park, Jerry."

Jerry grinned shyly. "You give me too much credit, Alex. Here's what we know so far." He indicated the wall monitor.

"These twelve GPS stations give us real time information about the different elevations, and what happened at Old Faithful was the only seismic event in the entire park. It's almost as if it was man-made. Any idea how that's even possible?"

Alex studied the monitor. It certainly was unusual for a seismic occurrence to happen in only one specific area, but the same thing had happened to Victoria, British Columbia, three weeks ago.

"I've heard stories about you, Alex. I'm not sure how much of it is true, but we have a mutual friend who thinks highly of you. Wesley Patterson. According to him, something caused an isolated seismic event to destroy Victoria. When I pressed him for an explanation, he said it would be up to you to explain what happened. So, what happened, Alex?"

"I know what you're thinking, Jerry, but the cause of the incident in Victoria is not what's causing the problem here in the park. At least, as far as I can see."

Alex thought about the situation for a moment. The Cold Energy operation was highly classified, but now he was curious if the two incidents might be related. "Send me all your data and I'll try to correlate it with my own research when I get home. If there's any kind of link, I'll let you know, but I wouldn't get my hopes up."

Jerry's shoulder's sagged. "At least now you know what's going on. Thanks for stopping by."

"Call me if anything changes."

Jerry stared after Alex when he turned and strolled out the door. He knew he was not telling him everything, so leaned back against the desk and crossed his arms. He stared across the room at the wall monitor, and the amber light from the GPS unit near the Old Faithful station was steady, so he grabbed his car keys off the desk on his way to the door.

Chapter 4

RUSSIA:

"Hit him again!" Boris Kinski ordered.

Sasha Kinski, Boris's sister, stepped back, lest the spattering blood from the man tied down to a wooden chair would stain her blouse. "I did not know a person could take this much punishment and still be alive."

The swelling around his eyes no longer allowed Brian Stone to see Rudolf Kinski's fist until it slammed against his face once again. His body was numb from the beating, and now he no longer felt the blows to his head.

"Where is Alex Cave's family?" Boris yelled.

In a drug-induced haze, Brian thought about the last time he had seen Boris's smug face. It was just before Alex had sliced a chunk of flesh from his cheek. A dark window closed around his thoughts, and Brian was grateful when his mind and body drifted into nothingness, and then his head fell limply against his chest.

"Check if he's dead." Boris ordered in nearly perfect English.

Rudolf took one of his bloodied gloves off and felt the artery on Brian's neck. "He is dead, Boris. Why are you still trying to kill Cave? You did the Russian way and kill brother for brother, and you still have me."

Boris suddenly leaned in close to Rudolf. "Look at me! I had women begging for my attention until Cave did this to my face. I was the head of the entire Russian Mafia until you recorded me killing those two CIA agents on your phone, you idiot! Now I'm a wanted man. Why couldn't Cave have killed you instead? All you're good for is causing pain. If you weren't my brother, I'd kill you!"

Boris looked at his younger sister. A tall, attractive brunette, quietly standing nearby. "Find out where Cave's family is located, Sasha. I'll make him watch them suffer for what he did to me."

Chapter 5

12:04 AM:

Just north of Mason, Wyoming, Alex turned east onto a two-lane road, but he kept thinking about what had happened at Yellowstone. For the Old Faithful geyser to erupt with such force meant something major had occurred deep beneath the park, but why had it erupted with such force and no warning bothered him.

The headlights illuminated a large green and white sign, welcoming him to Stillwater, Wyoming, population 950. Four-miles farther, he parked near the motel office and climbed out, and then stretched for a moment before entering.

A bell chimed as he walked through the swinging glass door, but there was no one behind the counter. He heard a television in the background, and a moment later, a Native American man walked out of an adjoining room.

"You must be Alex. I am Wasue. Okawna said you would show up this afternoon, but I did not think it would be this late."

Alex grabbed the registration pad and looked for a pen. "Sorry about that. I had to make an unexpected stop on the way."

Wasue held a key out above the registration form. "You need not bother with that, Alex. I know who you are."

Alex accepted the key and left the office, noticing his room was in front of his SUV. He grabbed his small suitcase from the back seat, opened the door, and flipped on the light switch as he walked into the modest room. He was dead tired, and just tossed the suitcase onto the dresser and set the alarm clock for 8:00 AM. Once undressed, he threw back the covers and collapsed onto the bed.

***

It seemed his head had just hit the pillow when blaring music of a country song erupted from the alarm clock. After a shower, he dressed and left his suitcase on the dresser, knowing he'd be staying at least another night.

He locked the door behind him and headed down to the office. When he stepped inside, the bell chimed and an attractive Native American woman in her late fifties walked in from the other room.

"Good morning, Alex. Is your room okay?"

"Yes, thank you. Do you know where I can get something to eat?"

"Yes, Arty's. It's the only restaurant for a hundred miles. Go right at the four-way stop, and it will take you through town. It's just down the street from the municipal building. The light in his sign is not working, but you can't miss it."

"Thanks. What do I owe you for the room?"

"Not a thing. My nephew considers you part of our family, and I'll see you at Ahiga's memorial service this afternoon."

Alex's eyebrow went up. "Ahiga? I thought his name was Richard?"

"Ahiga is his Indian name. It means he laughs, and Okawna means wolf, so his Indian name is Laughing Wolf"

Alex wondered why his best friend hadn't mentioned he was part Native American, and why his hair was blond instead of brown. "Then I guess I'll see you at the service. Thanks again."

Alex went outside and strolled back to his SUV, and then climbed in and rolled down the window as he started the engine. He drove down the highway into Stillwater, but when he turned right at the stop sign, he thought he had been transported back in time.

On the right side of the street, a row of two-story, red brick buildings were connected by a covered wooden walkway. One shop had an old barber's pole out front, and another had a large wooden scissors and a sewing thimble hanging out over the street. Farther down on his left, thick slabs of gray stone steps led up to the matching two-story Stillwater Municipal Building.

Alex saw the sign for Arty's restaurant and pulled into a parking spot near the front door, then shut off the engine. The aroma of bacon and coffee drifted through his window, and he smiled as he climbed out and took a moment to enjoy the magenta-colored sunrise over the wide-open desert.

When he opened the single glass door, a small bell chimed, and he smiled. It seemed everyone in this town had bells on their doors. He strolled inside and it could have been a scene from an old western movie. There were moveable round wooden tables and low back chairs, but no booths, and the long wooden counter reminded him of a bar in a saloon. He found a vacant table and sat down, and a moment later, a robust man with a slightly bulbous nose walked up to take his order.

"Good morning, Alex. I'm Arty. What can I get ya?"

"How did you know who I am?"

"It's a small community and people like to gossip."

Alex grinned. He liked the small town atmosphere, just like the little town where he grew up. "Bacon and eggs over easy would be nice."

"Will do. Would you like some coffee?"

"That would be great."

When Arty walked away, Alex stood to look at the pictures on the wall next to the counter. An old bronze framed photograph depicted an era of horse-drawn wagons and saddled horses tied to a hitching rail. Another picture showed the construction of the County Municipal building, with the year 1823 chiseled into an obelisk at the bottom of the steps. Another photo was looking down the main street at two vintage automobiles trying to get out of the muddy road.

One photograph showed the row of red brick buildings he had passed earlier, and the sign above the nearest store proclaimed the assayer's office was proudly owned by Wilber T. Patrick since 1807. Other photographs depicted the harsh conditions for the miners, and the gray mountain surrounding a mine entrance. He knew the pictures said a lot about the people in this community, and apparently, Stillwater was born as a mining boomtown, which had refused to die when the ore played out.

He walked back to his table and sat down just as Arty walked up and set his breakfast on the table. "Thanks."

"That earthquake yesterday sure shook up a lot of people around here. In fact, as far as I can remember, there has never been an earthquake here in Stillwater."

Alex's brows bunched together as he stared at Arty, thinking this can't be just a coincidence. "What time did it occur?"

"Right around two. I think it has something to do with what's going on at the old gold mine. One day, this big company from out west took it over, and nobody's been allowed to get close to it. A friend of mine said they're doing secret research for the government and they shoot trespassers."

Alex suppressed a grin. "I'll keep that in mind."

Alex finished eating and was sipping his coffee when the bell on the door chimed, and looked up as a stalky man wearing a tan police officer's uniform entered. The officer looked around for a moment and then walked up to his table.

"You must be Alex Cave. I'm Bruce Roswell, the County Sheriff. Mind if I join you?"

Alex indicated an empty chair. "Not at all, Sheriff."

Bruce slid the chair out and sat down across from Alex. "I understand you're a geophysicist."

"That's right."

Arty was listening and wanted to know more, so he grabbed an empty mug and a full pot of coffee. He hurried over and set them in front of the Sheriff and then took his time pouring before sitting down with them. "Don't mind me."

Bruce knew this would happen with Arty and continued. "Yesterday, there was a cave-in at the caverns because of the earthquake. Even though the caverns are open on the weekends, the State Park office is closed until Monday, and I was wondering if you could stop by and tell us if it's safe to let the tourists go down inside?"

Alex's curiosity was aroused, wondering if the earthquake and the collapse of the caverns could be connected to the incident in the park. It seemed impossible, because Yellowstone was two-hundred-miles northwest of this town. Still, it was worth considering the possibility. "I'll check it out after the funeral service."

"Of course, and I appreciate you taking the time on such a sad day. You'll drive past it on the way to the Okawna ranch."

"Who should I talk to at the caverns?"

"The Park Ranger, Philip Grady. Although it's not much of a park. Just a hole in the ground."

"All right. Arty was just telling me about the old gold mine. Do you know what's going on there?"

Bruce gave Alex a grim expression. "It used to be a government research facility before they suddenly shut it down, and then three years ago, it was leased to the DAR

Corporation. They did a lot of construction work in the area using outside contractors, but it wasn't reopened until a few weeks ago. They have their own security force, and I've run into a couple of them. I'm an ex-Marine, and I'll tell you what. Those guys aren't rent-a-cops. They're mercenaries."

"What's DAR stand for?"

"Demolition and Reconstruction. They do a lot of contract work for the Federal and State Governments after major disasters."

"I wonder why they would need a research facility."

"I couldn't say. Maybe they're going to mine the micro-gold." Bruce stood. "Thanks for the help, Mister Cave."

When the sheriff strolled out of the restaurant, Arty sat down across from Alex. "That's great that you're going to find out what happened. I still think it has something to do with the old gold mine. They're a shifty bunch, and the ones who occasionally stop in here for dinner look mean. Listen, this is a small town and I'm sort of the local news center. If you wouldn't mind, could you let me know what you find out?"

"Sure thing. I'll stop by on my way back."

When Arty got up and moved away smiling, he stood and left a nice tip. He headed over to the counter to pay for the meal and smiled at a sweet looking little gray-haired woman standing behind the antique cash register. He held out a twenty-dollar bill for the breakfast, but she just smiled.

"Thank you Alex, but breakfast is on Arty and me. I'm his wife, Rose."

"Thanks. This is a great place you have here. It reminds me of an old saloon."

"That's right. It used to be a saloon before Arty and I took over for my father, some forty-odd years ago. We had to upgrade the plumbing and electricity, but everything else is pretty much the same as when my grandfather first built it in

1826. He and his two older brothers were the first Patrick's immigrating to this area."

"Your husband seems like a nice fellow."

"Arty's a sweetheart, but you'll have to give him a little leeway when he tells you about something. There's no end to his imagination."

Alex glanced over and saw Arty laughing with some customers. "I'll do that, and thanks for the meal."

Alex strolled out the door, climbed into his SUV, and drove down Main Street. On his way back to the four-way stop, he slowed down as he drove past the municipal building to admire the architecture. It had an early western style, and the large blocks of cut gray stone used for the exterior gave it the look of permanence in an ever-changing world.

He continued down Main Street, noticing a small housing development behind the brick buildings, and thought it would be a nice place to grow up. It reminded him of his own small town in Washington State, and he thought perhaps that's why he and Okawna got along so well. They had worked together on secret missions for the CIA, and always had each other's backs, as if brothers. He turned right at the stop sign and headed toward the Okawna ranch.

Chapter 6

YELLOWSTONE NATIONAL PARK, MAMMOTH STATION, 9:25 AM.:

When Jerry hurried into the seismic center, Vivian swung her chair around to face him. "Old Faithful still hasn't erupted, and there isn't any seismic activity in the park."

Jerry stared at the display on the wall. "Old faithful has never failed to erupt, and I'm getting a bad feeling about all this. I'll call the Director of the National Park Service in Washington and let her know what's going on. If it were up to me, I'd start evacuating the park."

"It's nearly noon on the east coast, and it's a Saturday. She won't be at her office today."

Jerry knew Vivian was right, but something bad was going on in the park. His phone rang, and it was Paul. "Where are you?"

"I'm at the lake in Grant Village. We have a bunch of dead trout floating on the surface."

"I'm on my way."

***

Paul was standing on the dock, surrounded by a small crowd of tourists holding fishing poles. When he saw Jerry pull up in his SUV, he made his way to the shoreline across from the parking lot.

Jerry hurried across the wide lawn to Paul, who indicated dozens of fish belly up along the shoreline. He moved closer, recognizing several varieties of dead fish. "This is the strangest thing I've ever seen."

"Yeah, me, too. I've already packed a few specimens on ice for the biology specialists. A Park Ranger is coming to pick it up, and then I'll head back to the station."

Jerry's phone chimed, and he saw a text from Vivian, and then he looked up at Paul. "The alkali pools at West Thumb Geyser Basin are overflowing faster than normal, so I need to get over there."

"All right. Call me when you know anything."

"I will. I'll meet you back at the station."

Chapter 7

STILLWATER:

Alex drove for half an hour before seeing the sign for the Stillwater Caverns. When he saw the turnoff for the Cavern Visitor Center, he looked at the clock on the radio showing nine-fifteen. Since the funeral service was not until noon, he grinned and pulled onto the shoulder of the road to call Okawna.

"Hey, Alex. I heard you made it in late last night."

"I had to make an unexpected stop on the way. I told the sheriff I'd check on a cave-in at the caverns on the way back from the funeral, but I'm at the sign for the entrance right now, and I wondered if you would mind if I stopped here first?"

"No problem. It's early, and we're still trying to get organized, so take your time."

"All right. I'll see you when I'm finished."

In the distance were the nearly vertical gray stone mountains he had seen in the pictures, which were even more impressive in real life, so he was curious about how such an unusual formation would rise up in the middle of the desert. Being a geophysics instructor had its benefits, and all the geologic information he needed was on a hard drive.

He reached over the back seat to grab his computer and then brought up the information on this section of Wyoming. He learned the mountain resulted from an ancient volcanic eruption approximately sixty-five-million-years ago. He put it away and took the exit to the caverns and then drove east across the desert.

***

When he arrived at the visitor center, the only vehicles were a small sedan and a green Forest Service pickup. He parked near the front entrance and grabbed a flashlight from the back of his SUV before entering.

In the middle of the large circular room was a glass-covered display, and he walked over for a closer look. Under the glass was a three-dimensional representation of the tunnels and adjoining caverns below. He studied the displays on the walls, which gave a photographic history of the caverns and their discovery during the mining boom of the 1800s.

There was no one at the front desk, so he walked into the gift shop. He grabbed a tourist map of the caverns near the doorway and saw a young girl sitting behind the counter.

Sarah Marshall leapt out of her chair when a good-looking man walked in. "What can I do for ya, Mister?"

Alex noticed her name tag. "Hi, Sarah. I'm looking for Mister Grady."

"You must be the geology teacher. Philip said you'd be stopping by later this afternoon."

"I have some extra time, so I thought I'd stop by here first. Is that a problem?" He saw the girls shift her gaze to the doorway, and turned to look at a man wearing a dark green park service uniform.

Grady reached out to shake hands. "You must be Mister Cave. The sheriff said you'd be stopping by after the funeral, so this is a surprise. I was glad to learn there was a geophysicist in Stillwater. I don't think the damage is too dangerous, but since we've never had an earthquake before, it's nice to get a second opinion. Follow me and I'll tell you what happened."

Alex followed him around a corner and stepped into the elevator. According to the control panel, the only stops were at the top and bottom of the shaft.

Grady press the down arrow. "We'll be descending seven-hundred-feet below sea-level, so your ears are going to pop."

A few moments later, the doors opened, and Alex stepped out onto a concrete walkway. He followed Grady past several constructed side tunnels before they stopped at a natural opening of a tunnel into the rest of the cavern. It was nearly eight-feet-high and appeared to go on forever.

Grady saw Alex's surprised expression. "They found this opening four years ago, and it's amazingly straight for something natural. It's a mile long and ends at the cavern, so we have a long walk to get there."

Alex could tell Grady enjoyed his job, since he did not stop talking as they continued along the tunnel. He explained the different rock formations as if talking to a tourist, not a geophysicist. The tunnel sloped downhill at a shallow angle and it took fifteen minutes to reach the end, where a large area had been cut out of the rock, and concrete steps continued down to a lower level. The overhead lights were off, but a few battery-powered emergency lights dimly illuminated the room and steps.

Alex opened the tourist map and used his flashlight to show it to Grady. "Where are we exactly?"

Grady looked at the map and pointed to a spot. "Right about here. The cave-in occurred just around the corner at the bottom of the steps."

Alex grabbed his pen and made a few notes on the map. "How deep are we?"

"Just under eight-hundred-feet. Carlsbad Caverns are only sixty feet deeper than us."

The ghostly white beams from their flashlights danced around the tunnel, and the air had a familiar musty odor. The steps ended at an arched opening, and Alex followed Grady into a massive, oblong cavern. They stepped around stalagmites and pieces of stalactites broken loose from the ceiling as they slowly moved toward the opposite end, about two-hundred-feet further.

Alex pointed his flashlight overhead to study the damage. "This isn't too bad. The damage is mostly superficial."

He studied the sides of the chamber as they made their way back to the tunnel. "It looks like the worst of the cave-in is over, but I'm worried about these new fractures in the sides of the rock. There must be an aquifer nearby, or the water wouldn't be trickling out from the cracks so fast. You might have a problem with flooding down in these lower sections, so you should keep an eye on this area. I recommend having the engineers install a pumping system."

"I'll let my boss know on Monday. Are you ready to head back?"

Alex looked around the cavern one last time. "I've seen enough. Let's go."

***

When they stepped out of the elevator into the visitor center, Alex indicated the diorama of the caverns, and then walked over to look at it with Grady. "What's the scale of this model?"

"It's right over here on the placard. It's five hundred to one."

Alex knew the spread between the tip of his thumb and the tip of his little finger to be close to nine-inches, and used them to estimate the distance from the cave-in to the outside edge of the diorama.

Grady noticed the concerned look in Alex's eyes. "Is there something wrong with the display?"

"I'm not sure. It's just that the cavern is only fifteen-miles from the mine in the gray mountains the sheriff told me about."

"Do you think they caused the earthquake?"

"I can't imagine how."

"All right. Thanks for checking this out for me, Mister Cave."

"You're welcome."

Alex returned to his SUV and climbed into the driver's seat, but didn't start the engine and just leaned back to think. According to the diorama, the tunnel to the cavern and the town of Stillwater were in a direct line to the mine. He saved the location of the cavern in his GPS, and when he started the engine, the digital clock showed it was 11:47 AM. "Crap!"

He shoved the transmission into drive and raced out of the parking lot. When he reached the stop sign for the main road, he could see for miles in every direction, so didn't stop.

Chapter 8

USGS. YELLOWSTONE.

Vivian saw Jerry stroll into the office with fresh cups of coffee. "That's just what I need. I still can't find a reason for the tremor yesterday afternoon."

Jerry set one of the plastic mugs in front of her. "Paul checked out a report about the volume of water in the outflows of the lake and said it has increased significantly. I'm getting a bad feeling, Vivian."

"I know what you mean."

She noticed one of the GPS indicators on the map of the park suddenly begin flashing and typed the number into her computer. "That's the Thumb basin. The elevation just increased by half an inch."

More GPS warning lights flashed as Vivian typed the numbers into the computer. "They're coming from all the geothermal areas in the park."

Jerry grabbed his phone and entered Mira's number. After eight rings, he was about to hang up when she answered. "Are you all right?"

"Yes, but Old Faithful started erupting again, and it hasn't stopped. What should I do?"

"We have alarms going off all over the park, so tell everyone to leave."

"Of course. Thank you for calling. Please let me know what you find out."

"I will."

Jerry told Vivian what had happened. "I'm closing the park and we need to evacuate immediately. Let's make some calls."

Chapter 9

OKAWNA RANCH:

The asphalt ended abruptly, but the gravel road had been well maintained, and Alex continued at a decent speed. Barbed wire fences ran parallel to the road for several more miles until he saw two large posts supporting the dark wooden sign of the Okawna Land and Cattle Company.

He slowed down as he entered the large open graveled area between the main house and the outbuildings. Several vehicles were parked in the center area, so he parked on the end and climbed out.

He saw a small crowd of mostly Native American men, women, and children standing on the other side of the two-story house, so he quietly moved over to the outside edge of the group. Okawna had told him to dress casually for the funeral, and now he understood why. None of the men wore suits, only slacks or jeans and Native American shirts, and a few of the women wore patterned dresses or slacks and blouses, but most of them were dressed in Native American attire.

He saw the back of Okawna's tall, lean figure and shaggy blond hair standing in the front row of people. A tall woman with long, shiny black hair stood to his right, with a smaller blond-haired woman standing to his left side.

On the other side of a grave, he recognized the woman from the motel office wearing a long, white-leather dress and was clutching a tan-colored bag against her chest while speaking in a Native American dialect. A moment later, she stepped aside and Okawna walked forward to take her place.

When Okawna went to the other side of the grave to face his family and friends, he noticed Alex at the back of the crowd as he spoke to the group about his father. When he was finished, he stepped back to shake hands with everyone.

As the group broke up, Alex stepped out of the way and the dark-haired woman who had been standing next to Okawna moved through the crowd in his direction. When she stopped in front of him and held out her hand, he surmised she was in her mid-thirties, and attractive.

"You must be Alex Cave. I'm Fala Baldwin, Okawna's cousin."

Alex noticed the resemblance to the woman from the motel, but as he took her hand, he was nearly overwhelmed by a sense of Déjà vu. "Yes. That's right."

Fala noticed Alex's curious expression and wondered what he was thinking about, but didn't ask. "Okawna's description was rather vague, only that you were tall with wavy black hair. How long are you staying in Stillwater?"

"I'll be leaving tomorrow afternoon. I hope you don't mind my asking, but I noticed you called him Okawna. Does everyone in your family call him by his last name?"

Fala smiled. "Yes, even his mother. It's a family bet from when he was ten. Anyone who uses either of his first names has to pay him a dollar."

"He has two first names? I'd pay just to find out what they are."

Fala returned his grin and noticed Okawna moving in her direction. "Sorry, but he'll have to tell you."

Okawna walked over to Alex and gave him a quick hug. "I see you've met Fala."

Alex looked at her. "Is the woman from the motel your mother?"

"Yes. How did you know?"

"I see the resemblance, and you're both lovely women." He turned to Okawna. "Can we talk in private?"

Fala knew it was her cue to leave. "I'll see you two later."

When Fala turned and headed toward the back porch of the large house, Okawna noticed the corners of Alex's mouth rise into a grin as he stared after her. "She's divorced, in case you're interested."

"Am I that obvious?"

"It's about time you moved on, Alex. She's the main reason I wanted you to come to the funeral."

"I don't know if I'm ready for another relationship. Especially after Rita deceived me."

"I'm not trying to push you into anything, Alex. I just wanted you to meet her. She's Cherokee, in case you were wondering. Her mother named her Fala because of her black hair. In the native language, it means crow."

Alex watched Fala's trim figure climb the steps onto the back porch. When she disappeared into the house, he turned back to Okawna. "She is lovely. How come she's divorced?"

"Her ex used to live here in Stillwater and was one of the town's bad boys during high school. I tried to talk her out of marrying the bastard, but she wouldn't listen to me. The first time I saw her with a black eye, she said it was an accident, and wouldn't leave him. Two years ago, she got a restraining order from our local judge and filed for a divorce, but he refused to comply. A week later, he reconsidered and signed the papers, and hasn't come back."

Alex noticed a glimmer of satisfaction in Okawna's eyes. "A change of heart? I don't suppose you had anything to do with it."

"I might have made a subtle suggestion."

Alex smirked at him. "I've never known you to be subtle about anything."

"Yeah, well, you know me too well. What happened that made you arrive so late last night?"

Okawna listened as Alex told him about the stop at Yellowstone. "Did you find out what caused the cave-in at the caverns?"

"It appears to be from the same seismic event in the park, and that's what's bothering me. This area of Wyoming is geologically stable, and I can't explain the reason for the earthquake."

"We felt it here, too. Let's go inside and I'll introduce you to my mom."

When Alex walked into the house with Okawna, he saw Fala entertaining a little girl sitting in her lap. He was about to walk over to her when a small woman suddenly appeared in the walkway from the dining room.

Okawna walked over and put his arm around her shoulders. "Alex, this is my mom, Judith."

Alex hurried over and held out his hand. "It's nice to meet you, ma'am, and I'm sorry for your loss. I wish I could have met Richard."

Judith accepted his hand. "Thank you, Alex. Okawna has told me a lot about you. At least, what he's allowed to tell us. I think Richard would have liked you."

Alex smiled. "I'm sure Okawna told you what's important. I know Okawna means wolf, but if you don't mind me asking, what are his first names?"

Judith laughed. "I've already lost fifty dollars for saying it too often when he was a teenager."

"It's just one dollar each time, right? I'll cover it for you."

Fala stood and set the girl down on the chair, and then turned and smiled at Alex. "Judith named him Francis, after Saint Francis, and his second first name is Quanah, which Richard thought was funny. It means fragrant."

Alex looked over and grinned at Okawna's apparent embarrassment. "Now I know why he doesn't use it. I bet he had fun in high school."

Fala chuckled. "Yes, Okawna would throw the first punch when the white boys called him Francine, and did the same when he was called Fragrant Wolf by the Native boys."

Alex laughed, pulled out his wallet, and held a dollar bill out to him. "It's worth it, Francine Fragrant Wolf."

Okawna grinned and took the dollar. "And that's the last time you call me that, right?"

Alex gave him a smirk. "Sure thing, pal."

Fala liked the way Alex bantered with her cousin and moved closer to him as if it was the natural thing to do. She didn't understand why, but she felt as though they had known each other for some time. She turned and looked down at the young girl in the chair, who was staring up at Alex, so she nudged him in the side. "I think you have an admirer."

When Alex looked down at the little girl, she held her arms out to him. He wasn't sure what to do, so he looked at Fala for an answer.

"Alex, this is my daughter, Halona."

Alex hesitantly reached down and grabbed Halona under the arms. When he brought her close, she wrapped her arms around his neck as she sat on his forearm. He was surprised when she ran her fingers through his hair. "Hello, Halona."

Halona let go of Alex's hair and leaned back to look at his blue eyes. "Is your hair wavy all by itself?"

Alex looked around and noticed the stunned expressions on everyone's faces, and then gave Fala a questioning stare. "Did I do something wrong?"

Fala was intrigued. "Not at all. It's just that Halona is usually shy with strangers."

Alex smiled at Halona. "Yes, it does it all by itself. Is that why yours is so curly?"

"Yes. Mom says I get it from my Dad. I'm going to be six years old in three months and fourteen days."

Alex relaxed. He had not been around his niece very much when she was this young. When everyone moved into the dining room, he set Halona down and they followed them to a large wooden table, where Halona insisted on sitting between him and Fala. She also insisted on scooping potato salad from the bowl onto his plate, giving him far more than he wanted.

Alex had just finished eating when a tremor rattled the pictures in a nearby cabinet, and he saw everyone staring at him for an explanation. "I'm still trying to figure out the cause. Do any of you know what they are doing in the old gold mine?"

Okawna looked across the table at Alex. "No one knows what they do there."

"I wouldn't mind checking it out tomorrow before I leave."

"You won't be able to see anything. The mountain range is shaped like a narrow horseshoe, and the only way inside is at the open end. They have armed security guards at the entrance, and they won't let you in."

Fala had an idea. "I've been riding horses up the mountain range every summer since I was ten, and Uncle Richard taught me where to go. I can get you up to a lookout area on the rim of the mountain where you can see the entrance to the mine. It's only an hour's ride from here."

Judith reached over and put her hand on Alex's arm. "If those people at the mine are causing these earthquakes, you and Okawna need to shut them down. Richard and I built this ranch, Alex, and I won't sit by and let it be destroyed by those people."

Alex felt small fingers clasp his hand, so he smiled down at Halona. "There's no need to be afraid."

Halona slid off her chair and stood. "I'm not afraid." She pulled on his hand. "We need to sit outside after eating, Caveman."

Alex gave her a short laugh. "Caveman?"

Fala looked over at her daughter. "Why is he a caveman?"

"Because that's what Uncle Okawna calls him. He said it's because he likes rocks and his last name is Cave."

Okawna grinned when Alex looked at him. "I'd better go saddle the horses." As he walked out onto the back porch, he burst out laughing.

Alex followed everyone out onto the porch and stood near the railing, staring across the grasslands at the gray mountain range. He felt someone move up beside him and looked down at Halona as she pulled on his hand. He followed her over to a two-person chair and sat down then Halona climbed in and scooted over beside him. When he looked up at Fala, her eyes told him she was grateful for indulging Halona's forwardness, and he gave her a small smile.

Fala walked over beside Judith at the railing. "I miss him, too."

Judith took Fala's arm around her own. "Okawna is going to stay with me for a while. At least until I decide what to do with the ranch. Without Richard, I might have to sell it."

When Judith cried, Fala wrapped her arm around her shoulders. "There's no hurry. You just need some time to think about things. I'll stay here for a few more days, too."

Judith brought a tissue from her pocket and dabbed her eyes. Fala was like a daughter to her and Richard. "What do you think about Alex? Halona sure likes him."

"It's kind of strange, actually. It's as though I've known him for a while, but we've never met."

"Maybe it's because Okawna speaks so highly about him. Why don't you go sit with him for a while? Maybe you have met him before and just don't remember."

Fala walked across the porch and sat down on a chair facing Alex and Halona, and couldn't understand why her daughter had taken to him so quickly. "I know you and Okawna used to work for the CIA together, and I was wondering why you decided to become a teacher?"

"I had some personal issues to deal with and needed a change of occupation. I've always loved geology, and it seemed to be the right thing to do."

"It sounds like you're having second thoughts."

"To be honest, I'm bored to death. Where do you work?"

"I'm a veterinarian, and most of my work is with the animals in the park. That's why Halona and I live in West Yellowstone."

"Have you ever been to Bozeman, Montana?"

"No, I've never needed to go there."

"Perhaps I could show you and Halona the highlights sometime."

"That sounds nice."

"What's the story with Okawna's hair? He doesn't look like a Native American."

"Judith was already pregnant when she fell in love with Richard. Okawna's natural father, Jim Westmont, was a young Navy officer, and was killed in a training accident his second year out of the academy. Judith and Jim were best friends with my parents and Richard, and a few years later, they got married. Richard adopted Okawna and was a good father to him, and they loved each other immensely."

"Uncle Richard was funny." Halona piped in.

Okawna walked up the steps. "The horses are saddled, so whenever you two are ready, we can get going."

Alex walked beside Fala as they followed Okawna down the steps and around the house toward the barn, and he stopped at his truck to grab a set of binoculars. When they entered, the aroma of hay and manure reminded him of home.

Okawna indicated a large brown mare with a black mane to Alex. "I set the stirrup height the same as mine, so it should be close enough." He stroked the long jaw of his own dark brown stallion. "I raised this stud from a colt. He's a handsome devil, just like me."

Alex stepped into the stirrup and swung up onto the mare. "This works for me."

Once Okawna and Fala were ready, they rode out of the barn at a lope to let the horses get warmed up. A few minutes later, they were galloping across the desert.

When they reached the base of the mountains, Alex saw a few sparse areas of vegetation on the steep sides, but there were no trees, only ragged cliffs. Fala led them past an old rock quarry, where broken remnants of gray blocks lay scattered in discarded heaps.

Fala reined her horse to a stop. "The trail starts here, where they hauled drills and explosives to the top of the quarry to break up the rock."

Alex stared up at the side of the mountain. The stone appeared to be nearly vertical as it rose up toward the sky. If there was a way to the top, he couldn't see it.

When Fala began the assent, Alex followed behind her, with Okawna bringing up the rear. Some sections of the trail were solid rock and barely wide enough for the horses, with a vertical wall on one side and a sheer drop off on the other. Fifteen minutes later, they were forced to stop by a ten-foot tall, chain-link fence. Holes had recently been drilled into the rock and filled with concrete to anchor the support posts.

Alex raised his binoculars and stared down at what appeared to be an old volcanic crater. From his vantage point on top of the horse, he could see down into the tree-filled valley below, and the entrance into the mine appeared to be tiny. "Are you sure this place is occupied? I don't see any vehicles, and the open area in front of the mine looks like it hasn't been driven on in years."

Fala turned her horse around to look at Alex. "This is as close as we're going to get"

"I'll try to find out what they might do here."

There was only enough room for the horses to turn around, so they began their descent in reverse order, with Okawna leading the way.

***

COBRA:

Rita had agreed to stop her experiments, and so far, the seismic events had ceased, which gave credence to Henry's theory their tests had been the cause. The only problem was until the other device arrived, there was little to occupy her time.

Henry kept thinking about the laboratory below, and the massive steel door at the entrance, then looked across the dining table at Chris, who was reading a magazine. "Do you have the key for the elevator that will allow us to go down to the lowest level of the facility?"

Chris looked up at Henry. "Yeah, but there isn't anything down there. Just a big safe in the floor."

That got Rita's attention, and she looked up from her laptop computer. "I'd like to see it."

Chris shrugged and stood from the table. "I'll go get the key."

Henry slid his chair back and stood. "I believe we may find an answer to why this facility was sealed."

Rita closed the laptop and got up from her chair. "I was searching the Internet for any information about this place, but I can't find anything except it was a gold mine. Either the people that worked here were all sworn to secrecy, or they're all dead."

Chris walked into the lounge from the living quarters. "Let's go."

The trio walked across the main room and entered the elevator, where Chris inserted the key, gave it a quarter turn, and pressed the button for the bottom floor. When the cab began dropping, Henry noticed the indicator light for the third floor blinked off. When he felt the pressure against his eardrums increase, his anxiety level also rose. For him, it felt like an hour passed before the elevator car slowed to a stop and the doors opened.

Chris stepped out first and flipped the light switch. Three rows of eight-foot long fluorescent lights on the ceiling fluttered in the darkness before bursting into bright white light.

When Henry and Rita stepped out, Chris waved his hand down at the six foot square steel vault door in the concrete floor. "They welded the door closed, so whatever is in the vault must be top-secret." He pointed up at a large metal hook secured to the concrete ceiling. "That's directly over the vault, so they must have used it for hauling something in and out of the hole."

When Henry looked at Rita, he noticed the concern in her eyes. "You must allow me to call Director Donner. We must find out what is buried down there."

Rita crossed her arms. "As I explained to you before, once he knows where we're, he'll storm this facility. I'm not looking forward to being locked in a cell."

"I will not press charges against you, Rita. Just get me out of this bomb shelter."

Rita stared at him. "This isn't a bomb shelter, Henry."

Henry sighed. "Of course. My mistake."

From the tone of Henry's voice, she could tell he was extremely agitated. "What happened to you?"

Henry was about to explain when the concrete seemed to lurch up beneath them, throwing them off balance. He toppled over, crashing onto the floor as Rita and Chris dropped on to their hands and knees. It was over quickly and everything was still, but then alarm horns blared from the elevator shaft.

Rita and Chris hauled Henry to his feet and dragged him into the cab. Chris stabbed his finger against the button for the top floor, hoping it still worked. When the door closed, they felt the car rising up the shaft, and then the volume of the alarm increased as they passed the second floor. When the doors finally opened on the main floor, the first thing they saw straight across the room was the massive steel door closing.

Chris reached down and grabbed Henry up into his arms as he and Rita ran for the opening. The ever-narrowing gap seemed miles away, and then a heavy thud sound echoed across the room as the door slammed shut. They continued running, desperately hoping the locking bolts had not slid into place, but before they arrived, the green light above the door blinked out, and the red light came on.

"Shit!" Chris yelled as he stopped and set Henry down.

Henry stared at the door and up at the ceiling, and his lower lip trembled as he slowly lowered himself onto the floor. He felt like a little boy trapped in the bomb shelter.

Rita noticed Henry was shaking and knelt down beside him. When he looked up at her, the fear in his eyes broke her heart. She gently wrapped her arms over his shoulders and pulled him close against her chest. She felt him shaking with fear as she listened to his deep sobbing, realizing it was her fault, and rocked him in her arms.

***

THE MOUNTAIN:

Fala's horse reared up as the mountain seemed to lurch into the air. She managed to hang on to the horn, but as the horse came down, its front legs slid over the edge of the trail, dragging her down the mountain.

When Alex watched Fala and the horse toppling down the side of the mountain, he leapt off his horse and jumped over the edge. The heals of his shoes slid across the flat gray stone as he leaned back against the surface for balance.

Fala's foot was trapped in the stirrup and she struggled to get free as the sliding horse dragged her down the mountain. They both suddenly bounced into the air and her foot slipped out, but then she saw the horse fly over a cliff. She rolled over onto her stomach and dug her fingers along the rock, desperate for something to grab before slipping over the edge.

As he continued sliding down the rock, Alex stared in numbed silence as the horse vanished from sight. When Fala suddenly disappeared, his heart nearly stopped. "No!" He yelled as he continued sliding down the mountain.

As her torso slid over the edge, Fala's right fingers suddenly dug into a crack in the rock. The pain in her knuckles from the sudden weight brought tears to her eyes, yet somehow she hung on. When Halona's smiling face flashed through her mind, she gritted her teeth, forcing all her willpower to the tips of her fingers as they lost strength. She knew it was only a matter of seconds before she could no longer hang on, so she whispered an Indian prayer for Halona.

When Alex noticed the flesh color on the edge of the cliff, he pressed his palms hard against the surface to slow down. He slid to a stop at the edge of the cliff, rolled over onto his side, and reached out to grab the set of fingers clinging to the edge of a small crack. When he saw the fingers sliding loose, Alex lurched forward over the edge.

Chapter 10

THE CAVERNS:

Both Grady and Sarah felt a shudder in the floor, and then everything was still. Grady went through each room to check for damage, but didn't see anything unusual, but when he returned to the reception area, the odor of sulfur hung in the air.

Grady stepped into the gift shop and Sarah looked at him and scrunched up her nose. "What is that stink?"

"It's sulfur. I think it's stronger in the reception area, so I'll go try to find the source."

The odor led him to the elevator shaft, so he pressed the button to open the door. A thin cloud of steam roiled toward his face, so he turned and hurried into the gift shop. "Something is going on down below, so I'm going to check it out."

"Didn't you notice it earlier when you were down there with Mister Cave?"

"No, but that last earthquake might have caused more damage to the cavern. I'll be right back."

***

When the door opened at the bottom, Grady stepped out into a sauna. He heard a faint hissing sound and followed the noise as he moved along the walkway. It seemed to come from the tunnel leading to the cavern, so he headed in that direction.

Drops of perspiration dripped from his forehead, and by the time he reached the entrance to the cavern, his clothes stuck uncomfortably on his skin. The hissing was coming from inside the room, but he didn't understand how it was possible, since the cavern was nowhere near a heat source.

He was about to step inside when the hissing grew louder, slowly rising in pitch as if building up pressure. He turned and ran back up the tunnel, but it seemed to take forever to reach the elevator and he jabbed his finger against the button.

It seemed to take forever for the door to open and spun around with his back up against it. The pressure built up against his eardrums and he did not hear the ding of the bell as the door opened, but the sudden drop in pressure hurled him backward against the rear wall of the cab. His skin felt on fire as he slid to the floor and curled into a ball. He tried to scream, but his lungs were seared by the scalding steam before everything went black.

***

When Sarah heard a hissing noise coming from the reception area, she slowly crept across the floor to the elevator. The bell dinged, and when the door opened, she screamed and jumped back while staring at Grady on the floor. His skin was the color of a boiled lobster and covered in blisters. Steam shot out from around the cab and she ran from the building.

She made it to her car, only then realizing her keys and phone were in her purse in the gift shop. She did not have a spare, so she ran over to Grady's Park Ranger pickup, threw open the door, and jumped in. The key was not in the ignition, so she yanked the visor down, but nothing dropped out. When she looked back at the building, it was hidden in a cloud of steam, so she toppled out and ran from the parking lot, hoping someone would find her when she reached the main road.

Chapter 11

YELLOWSTONE:

Jerry drove into the parking lot at the Thumb Geyser Basin and climbed out of his car as a park ranger ran up to him. "What's going on, Jim?"

"I've never seen so many geysers erupting at the same time, Jerry. It's as if they are synchronized to erupt at the same instant. What is happening to the park?"

"The caldera is becoming active. Didn't you get the word to evacuate?"

"Yes, a little while ago."

The ground suddenly heaved up and car alarms blared in the parking lot. They both turned to look when they heard screams of agony and panic, and could only stare helplessly as scalding water rained down on the tourists running along the wooden walkways.

Jerry heard Vivian's voice yelling his name and grabbed the portable radio. "I'm here."

"The GPS alarms are going off all over the place. The seismic detectors are showing four-point-seven magnitude earthquakes covering a fifty-mile radius outside the park. All indications show an eruption is imminent, Jerry. What do you want me to do?"

"The phone number for Wyoming's Governor is in my computer. Tell her if Yellowstone erupts, thirteen hundred square miles of the surface will be instantly vaporized, so she needs to activate the emergency broadcast system and organize mass rescue operations outside the park."

"I will. What are you going to do?"

Jerry looked up into Jim's imploring eyes and then spoke into the radio. "We have too many injured people here, so I'm staying to lend a hand. Find the phone number and get out of there right now. You can call the governor from your cellphone."

"I will."

Jerry looked up at Jim. "Let's organize the people who can still drive into an ambulance service. Have them take the injured with them before they drive away."

As Jim stopped the people running to their vehicles, Jerry moved to the back of his car to retrieve the emergency medical supplies. Even though he knew within a year of an eruption, it wouldn't matter who he saved today, he would try to ease their suffering.

Chapter 12

COBRA:

Once Henry had recovered from his anxiety, Rita stood and stepped in front of the keypad for the door. When she realized she didn't even know the combination, she turned and gave Chris a pleading look.

Chris knew what she wanted. "One, nine, seven, four, six."

Rita tapped the numbers into the control pad and waited, but nothing happened, so she turned back to Chris. "Are you sure?"

"That's the number they gave me, but I've never tried it."

Rita turned back to the control pad and jabbed her fingers against the buttons. When nothing happened, she slammed her fist against the wall. "Open, damn it!"

Chris knew it was a waste of time, as he reached down to help Henry up off the floor. "Let's go to the lounge."

Henry felt his face flush with embarrassment. "I apologize for my childish behavior. It is a mental wound that will not heal."

Chris smiled at him. "It scared the hell out of me too, Henry."

Rita followed them across the room into the lounge and sat at the table with Henry. "I'm really sorry about all this. I never intended to put you in danger."

Henry stared at her for a long moment while he thought about what had happened below. "These devices will be the death of us all, Rita. As a species, we are too inept to deal with such advanced technology. I wish we would never have found them."

Chris had continued into the kitchen. When he returned, he set three cans of soda on the table and sat down.

Rita opened her can and took a sip. "What bothers me now is the earthquake happened without us using the device. We're not in control anymore."

When she saw the panicky look in Henry's eyes, she reached over and squeezed his hand. "This facility appears to be handling the stress, so I don't expect it to collapse on us."

Even mentioning the word collapse sent a shiver up Henry's spine. "Surely someone will come looking for us."

Chris suddenly stood from the table. "All the hard-wired phone lines were removed for security reasons and we don't have cellphone service because of the mountain, but we have wireless internet."

He hurried across the room and grabbed his laptop off the kitchen counter. Once he sat back down, he opened the cover and typed in his password. "I can't get a signal. It must be because the door is closed. The transmitter and receiver unit is camouflaged out near the tree line."

Henry suddenly remembered what Chris had told him about the security. "What about those roving guards? Surely they will notice the door is closed."

"They never come down the tunnel unless we ask them to." He looked at Rita. "When is Preston supposed to return?"

"Not until the other device arrives, and I have no idea how long it will take to get it here."

Chris suddenly looked up at the ceiling. "Do you hear that?"

When they shook their heads, Chris pointed at the ventilation duct. "The air conditioning has shut down. It might have something to do with the door sealing us inside.

Whatever they were doing in this facility, they didn't want it to get out."

Henry clasped his hands together in his lap to keep them from shaking. The haunting memory of being trapped in the bomb shelter would not go away.

Chapter 13

THE MOUNTAIN:

Alex barely managed to grab Fala's wrist as his chest stopped just before he went over the edge. "Reach up and grab my arm!"

When Fala felt a hand crushing her wrist, she looked up and Alex was staring down at her, his face a mask of desperation. She summoned all her strength and threw her free arm up toward Alex, but missed his arm by mere inches. She heard Alex groan under the added strain and knew she only had enough strength for one more try. She clenched her teeth as she swung her arm up toward Alex and her fingers tightened around his wrist.

Alex's other hand was all that was keeping him from sliding over the edge, but he could tell Fala was not going to climb up on her own. If he released his other hand to help her, they would both slide over the edge.

When her hand lost its grip, he knew he had no choice. He let go of the rock and reached down to grab Fala's coat collar, barely getting a grip as she slid over the edge of the cliff. He suddenly felt his belt dig into his stomach as he stopped sliding, but his only thought was to drag Fala up over the edge. As he pulled on her coat collar, the rest of her coat held tight to her body and he dragged her up to his shoulders. "Reach up and grab my belt!"

Fala stretched as far as she could, barely managing to slip her fingers around the thick leather strap near Alex's stomach and she hauled herself up over his hips, only then noticing Okawna straining to hang on to Alex's belt. Once her knees were over the edge, she rolled to one side and sat on her butt.

Alex was still face down as he was pulled back from the edge. Once on solid ground, he rolled over and stared at Okawna's grim expression. "Thanks buddy."

"I was in the area." He looked over at his cousin. "Are you hurt?"

Fala held up her fingers and her fingernails were ripped and bleeding. "I can't feel the tips yet, but I'll be all right."

The trio remained seated as they waited for the adrenalin to flush out of their systems, then Fala leaned forward and kissed Alex on the cheek. "Thank you."

Alex looked over the edge and saw the bloody body of the horse two-hundred-feet below, and was grateful his friend had his back. He leaned back and released a long sigh of relief as he looked at Fala. "I'm sorry about your horse."

Okawna stood and reached down to help Alex and Fala up from the ground. "Let's get back up to the horses before they leave without us."

They carefully climbed back up the steep rock face and found the two horses staring down at them. Alex climbed onto his mare and reached down to help Fala up behind him. Once Okawna was settled on his stallion, they continued down the mountain.

***

They rode the horses into the barn and Fala slid off from behind Alex. "I'll go check on Halona and Judith."

Alex climbed off and began removing the saddle. "Something under that mountain is causing these seismic events."

"Talk to Spencer at the assayer's office in Stillwater. He knows this area pretty well. He and his family have owned the business since the town was founded."

"My first class isn't until 1:00 PM on Monday, so I'll talk to him first thing in the morning on my way home."

As they headed back to the house, Alex stopped at his car to grab his cellphone. "I'll call Martin and find out what they were doing in the mountain."

"It's Saturday. I doubt he'd be at work."

"I have his private number."

Alex placed the call as they walked up onto the porch, and he saw Fala and Halona sitting in a chair next to Judith. Donner finally answered. "Sorry for calling you at home, but I need your help again." He explained his suspicions about the earthquakes and the DAR Corporation leasing the facility. "Do you know anything about them?"

"Yes, I do, and things are starting to make sense now. Before I went home last night, I was informed Rita is working for Steve Preston, the owner of the DAR Corporation. There's a good chance they took the device and Doctor Heinz to that facility. I don't know why they shut it down, but I'll find out on Monday and call you."

"Thanks, Martin."

Alex explained everything to Okawna. "If they have Henry, I'm sure he's scared right now. He has a problem with being underground."

Alex took a moment before deciding what to do. "I have to get him out of there."

He looked at his watch and it showed 3:37. "Does Spencer work on Saturdays?"

"Yes, but he usually leaves at 4:00. I'll call and ask him to wait for you."

"Thanks. I'll drive back to town and call you once I have a better idea of what I need to do to get inside."

"Let me know if you need any help."

"I will."

He walked down the steps and over to his SUV. When he looked back, Fala and Halona had gotten up and were staring at him. He waved and climbed in and then drove out below the sign for the Okawna Land and Cattle Company.

Chapter 14

STILLWATER:

Alex parked in front of an old red brick building with a sign for Spencer Patrick, Assayer. The front door was open, so he stepped through into a page out of history. Beautifully handcrafted oak cabinets covered the walls, and the door of a large vintage vault hung open in the back of the room. A black-walnut desk occupied the center of the room, supporting the legs of the bald man sleeping in the high back leather chair, so Alex cleared his throat.

Spencer Patrick opened his eyes and saw the figure of a person on the other side of his desk. He grabbed his steel-rimmed glasses off the top, put them on, and then looked up at a tall man smiling down at him. "Sorry about that. I didn't hear you come in. You must be Alex."

"Yes, and thank you for waiting for me. I'm interested in that old gold mine in the gray mountain."

Spencer smiled as he stood and shook Alex's hand. "Everyone calls me Spencer. I heard you were in town for the funeral. If I remember correctly, you're a geophysics instructor."

"That's right. I teach at the college in Bozeman."

Spencer walked to one cabinet to grab a large rolled-up map from a shelf. "It's interesting you arriving, just as these geological incidents are occurring. This is what you're looking for."

Spencer spread the faded gray paper across the desk, placing two small brass horse-head weights on either side to hold it open. Alex studied the map, noticing someone had meticulously drawn a mountain range in the shape of a horseshoe, including the elevations at different points around the rim and the length and width of the valley inside.

Spencer gave Alex a conspiratorial grin. "You know what it is, don't you?"

"Yes. It's the crater of an ancient volcano."

"My thoughts exactly. I'm interested in geology, too. I'm just an amateur with no formal training, but when you grow up in a mining community, you pick up a few things here and there."

"If the mine is played out, what supports the town's economy?"

"The ranchers, mostly. I pay for the community services myself. My great grandfather found three significant ore deposits in the area and died a very rich man. He was a shrewd businessperson and set up trust funds for his blood descendants. Now my brother and I are the only ones left. Arty's happy with running his restaurant, and I'm happy doing whatever I want, like searching for minerals. I've never been the materialistic type, and this town is my home, and I just want to help keep it going. They made me the Mayor, but I don't do much politically. I'm just a figurehead and let the people in the municipal building take care of running the town."

Alex pointed at the inside of the rounded end of the horseshoe. "Is this the entrance of the mine?"

"Yes. The gold played out back in 1846, and no one has tried again."

"Do you know when the government took it over?"

"It was back in 1964. That's when I met my wife. She was one of the scientists working on the project until 1970, when they abandoned the facility and sealed it closed."

"Do you know what they did there and why they closed it down?"

"Yes. During the Apollo missions, the government realized if they managed to get to the moon and back, they could bring home some rocks, and needed a place to isolate and study any organisms found in the samples. In 1964, they converted the mine into the research facility and called it COBRA. It was also the perfect place to tap into the geothermal energy, so they installed a steam-powered turbine generator. They used transistors for the electronic control system, which were state-of-the-art at the time."

"That makes sense. What happened?"

"It seems one sample they brought back from the moon was actually some kind of green meteor. They took it to COBRA to run tests, but once it was exposed to the atmosphere, the meteor's temperature increased and it was melting through every known material. Ceramic seemed to slow it down, so they encased it in clay and used the meteor's own heat to turn it into a massive ceramic ball. They lowered the whole thing to the bottom of an eight hundred foot deep mineshaft and filled it in with concrete."

"Didn't anyone return to find out if the meteor had melted through the ceramic ball?"

"through the ceramic ball?"

Spencer shrugged his shoulders. "The project was classified Top Secret, so maybe it was forgotten."

"Or, the project was covered up in a mountain of paperwork, if you'll forgive the pun. Especially if it was some politician's pet project."

"That would have been Jack Carter. He was the congressional representative for Wyoming back then. He was the one who made the proposal to build the facility in the old mine."

Alex looked down at the map. "So, the only way into the valley is here at the open end of the rim?"

"That's right."

"Do you have a map showing the layout of the mining operation?"

"Several. How far back?"

"When the mine was shut down. I need to see the layout of the tunnel system they dug into the mountain."

Spencer had worked in the office since he was ten and knew the location of every document from memory, and it only took a second to locate what Alex was looking for. "This is the last recorded drawing before the mine shut down, and I remember because my grandfather drew this one. He was handed a stack of hand-drawn pictures and had to figure out a way of drawing it to scale."

Alex watched and listened while Spencer pointed and described the different areas of the drawing. "This is the main entrance into the mine. You can see by the scale it was only wide enough for an ore-cart until it goes into this large open area. That's where they found the mother lode of gold. These side tunnels off the main area were exploratory shafts, but they didn't find enough gold to make it worthwhile back then."

Alex noticed a long, thin line running from the main chamber to the outside of the mountain, and pointed it out to Spencer. "What does that represent?"

"It's a ventilation shaft. This mark near the main chamber means it collapsed just before they shut it down. Is there anything else you'd like to see?"

"Yes, a better picture of the Stillwater Caverns. All I have is a tourist map."

Spencer understood and pulled an old diagram from a drawer and handed it to Alex. "You can keep that one. I have more copies."

"I discovered water seeping into the main cavern, and Grady told me it wasn't there until after the cave-in. How deep is the water table in this area of Wyoming?"

"Let me show you."

Alex's phone rang, and he recognized the ID. "Hey, Jerry. Did something happen in the park?"

"How did you know?"

"I'm in Stillwater, Wyoming, and we had a major seismic event here about three hours ago, so whatever is happening here is affecting your park. How bad was it?"

"All indications are this volcano is becoming active, so I'm evacuating the park."

"I'm trying to find out the reason for this sudden activity, and I'll call you if I learn anything new."

"Try to learn fast, Alex. I don't like where this is headed. If these earthquakes continue, this volcano is going to explode."

"All right."

Alex told Spencer what was going on. "I've got to figure out why this is happening."

Spencer dragged another map from the cabinet and rolled it out on the desk. It showed the layout of the western plains of the US, and he indicated the area southeast of Stillwater. "This is the Ogallala reservoir, about three hundred feet under the Great Plains."

Alex noticed one long, slender blue arm branching off in a northwest direction. "What's that called?"

"It's not called anything. It's just an extension from the reservoir where we get our water from the wells. It also drains down when it reaches Yellowstone. This is where some of the water for the hot springs comes from."

"Do you have some detailed maps of the rock strata between Stillwater and Yellowstone National Park?"

Spencer opened one of the lower doors in the cabinet. He shuffled through a few maps, grabbed a flat one, and set it on the desk.

Alex's phone rang, so he turned to stare out the window. "Hi, Martin. I'm surprised you called me back so soon."

"I've just received a report they are evacuating Yellowstone because of a possibility it might erupt. I wanted to check to see if you know anything about it."

"I sure do. The head geologist called a few minutes ago, and I believe there is a good possibility."

"Damn. All right. I'm on my way to my office to meet with the President's Chief of Staff, so I'll tell him what we suspect will happen."

"I'm trying to get inside, but they have a private security force guarding the entrance."

"I can get a squad of Marines headed in your direction."

"I don't have time to wait. If I don't stop these earthquakes, Yellowstone is going to erupt."

"How can the park be reacting to the earthquakes in Stillwater? It's hundreds of miles away."

Alex felt a hand on his arm and looked down at Spencer. "What is it?"

Spencer pointed at the map on the desk showing the rock strata. "This is the best one I have."

Alex studied the map for several moments before he spoke to Martin. "That's what I was afraid of."

"What's that?"

"Steam, Martin. If the meteor cracked through its ceramic shell, it could be super-heating the underground aquifer system. If it flash boils the water into steam, it would fracture the surrounding rock strata. That's what is causing the earthquakes."

"I still don't get the connection."

"There is a fifty-mile diameter pocket of magma below Yellowstone, and if enough steam pressure is forced against the pocket, the magma will have only one place to go, and that is up. Yellowstone National Park will turn into the largest volcanic eruption humanity has ever seen. The ash cloud will reach forty-miles into the atmosphere, and everything within a five-hundred-mile radius of the eruption will be instantly destroyed. No one will escape its destruction, and every living thing on the surface will die."

"I'll make some calls and get you some support."

"I can't wait, Martin. I might have a way for me and Okawna to get inside, so I'll be unreachable once we start."

"I'll get reinforcements heading in your direction, just in case they're needed."

"Thanks."

Spencer waited until Alex ended his call. "Need any help?"

Alex knew taking Spencer with them would just be another person for him to worry about. "You could show me how to open up the ventilation shaft and I'll take it from there."

"I know where I can get a few sticks of dynamite, and I've been hankering to blow something up. There's an old road on this side of the mountain below the shaft, and I'll lead the way."

Spencer's cellphone rang, so he answered. A moment later, he looked at Alex. "The sheriff wants to talk to you. He's waiting for you in the municipal building, so you go ahead and I'll go get the dynamite."

"Okay. I'll call Okawna and have him meet us there."

***

Alex parked in the visitor section, and as he climbed out, he recognized the obelisk from the picture and headed up the steps. When he walked through the swinging double doors, he saw a gray-haired woman sitting at the front desk, talking on the phone. She smiled and pointed to his right, so he walked down the hallway, and the last door had COUNTY SHERIFF painted in black letters on the frosted window.

He was about to knock when he heard Bruce holler to enter, so he opened the door and stepped into the room. "I got your message, Sheriff."

"Have a seat, Alex. I have people calling in from all over the county wondering what's going on, but I don't know what to tell them."

"I think I finally know why you're having the earthquakes." He told Bruce everything he knew, and his plan to get into the facility. "Okawna's on his way here to help me."

"Are you sure that's a good idea? I mean, all you have is a theory that they have the device you mentioned."

Alex stared at Bruce for a moment. "Perhaps, but I am positive the mine is the epicenter for these seismic events. I have to get inside the facility to find out why and stop it."

"All right, but no sense blowing things up just yet. Let me call George and we'll check out the entrance from his helicopter first."

"That works for me. How long until he can get over here?"

"We can be at his office in a couple of minutes by car. Spencer lets him use the movie theatre as an office and landing pad."

"It will take Okawna at least an hour to get here."

"Like I said this morning. I've met a couple of the guards, and since you're the expert, they might let us in."

"It's worth a try."

Bruce made the call to George, while Alex called Spencer and Okawna to let them know what they were doing. Spencer said he would get the tools they might need to get inside the mountain, and will meet them at the theatre when they got back.

Chapter 15

MOVIE THEATRE:

Bruce parked his patrol SUV next to the building, and then he and Alex climbed out. They heard the familiar whine of the turbine engine as they strolled over to a metallic green Bell helicopter, and the slender man standing beside it.

"Alex, this is George Whitley."

Alex shook his hand. "That's a nice bird you have. I've flown one myself."

George grinned. "It's always nice to meet a fellow pilot. Let's go."

They all climbed in, with Alex in the copilot seat, and then the helicopter leapt off the ground. Alex stared out the window as George swung it around on a northerly heading.

***

Ten minutes later, George flew the helicopter over the southern rim of the mountain so Alex could get an aerial view. He clearly saw the outline of a volcanic crater, and the entire area inside was forested, except for the small area in front of the mine, and the opening at the other end of the horseshoe.

George flew them to the northern end of the crater, where they could barely see the two green rooftops of the guard shack and barracks hidden in the trees. Once past the tree line, he kept the helicopter hovering above the turnaround area of the clearing.

Three men with holstered pistols walked out from the trees and waved him down in a friendly manner, so George looked over at Alex for approval. "It's your call."

"They might help us get inside, so land."

George put his bird down in the widest area and set the engine to idle as his passengers climbed out. He remained inside with the rotor blades still spinning in case they needed to get away in a hurry.

Bruce led Alex away from the slight downdraft and recognized one man. "Rick Daniels, this is Alex Cave, a geophysicist. He believes something inside the facility is causing these earthquakes. Can you tell us what they're doing in there?"

"I can't say, because I don't know, but I'm glad you came, Sheriff. After that last earthquake, I tried to call Preston, but I couldn't get through. I sent one of my people down the tunnel to the entrance, but the door was shut. I told him the entry code, but it didn't work."

Alex knew one way to verify his suspicions. "Do you know what they took into the facility?"

Daniels studied Alex for a moment. "Yeah, but I can't tell you for security reasons."

"I understand your reluctance, but if I'm correct about what's inside that place, it's causing these seismic events and things will get much worse. I know it was something similar to a torpedo, and if I don't get inside to stop it, Yellowstone could erupt."

Daniels could tell Alex was serious. "All right. Last weekend, this red-haired woman and an old man arrived, and we unloaded this big ass torpedo, like you said. They took it inside, and we were told to return to our station. Preston stops by once in a while, but that's all I know about it."

"Why would they shut the door?"

"That's just it. They wouldn't. That door is never closed."

"Is it okay if we fly in and check it out?"

"I'll go with you."

George waited while Bruce and the stranger climbed into the back seat and looked over at Alex as he climbed into the co-pilot's seat. "A new friend?"

"For now. I really appreciate your help with this, George. Could you take us to the mine entrance?"

George shoved the throttle forward, took off from the field, and headed toward the other end of the crater. "What's this all about, Alex?"

Alex turned in his seat so Daniels could hear him too and gave a brief description of the original purpose of the facility. When George asked him who had built the device, Alex knew he couldn't tell him the truth. "That's all I can tell right now."

A few moments later, George brought the helicopter over the entrance. When he gently touched down on the landing area, he and Alex were the first to notice no dust bellowing up from the ground.

Alex opened his door and stepped out. "It's no wonder we didn't see any vehicle tracks when we flew over earlier. It's painted concrete."

Once the others climbed out, Daniels led the way to the entrance, but the overhead lights were off, casting the interior into gloomy darkness. He pulled a penlight from his shirt pocket and aimed it down the tunnel, and was about to enter when he felt a hand on his shoulder, so turned to look at George. "What?"

"Hold on a second, I've got a lantern in my bird."

George ran back to the helicopter. When he returned with the bright light, they headed down the tunnel, and no one spoke until they arrived at the door.

Daniels indicated the control panel. "This key pad should be illuminated."

He entered the code anyway and nothing happened, so he turned to look at Alex. "We can't get in."

"How thick is that door?"

"It's two feet of hardened steel, Mister Cave. Even ten pounds of C-4 wouldn't blow a hole in it. There is just no way we can get inside."

Alex turned to Bruce. "I guess we go with plan b."

When everyone turned and hurried back along the tunnel, Alex borrowed the pen light from Daniels and aimed it at the ceiling and walls as they continued to the opening. He was relieved there were no noticeable cracks, and once they stepped out of the entrance, he gave it back.

Daniels saw one of his men waiting nearby in a brown and green SUV. As he hurried over to talk to him, he noticed the man seemed nervous. "What's going on?"

"We just found out they are evacuating Yellowstone Park. After what that Cave person told us, the rest of the guys left the area. All the other vehicles are gone, so I came to get you. We should leave this place."

Daniels walked over to the others standing outside the helicopter and repeated what he was told. "I'm leaving with my men. Good luck."

When Daniels turned to leave, Alex, Bruce, and George climbed into the helicopter and took off, headed back to Stillwater. Alex called Okawna and Spencer to let them know they couldn't get inside and would meet them at the rendezvous point.

***

As George approached the theater parking lot, they saw a large white pickup with oversize tires parked next to Bruce's patrol car. Once they set down, everyone climbed out.

Alex went over to Okawna and Patrick, who were standing near the big truck. "Nice play toy, Spencer."

"It sure is. I've got everything you need in the back, Alex."

Bruce reached out to Okawna. "Sorry about your dad."

Okawna accepted. "Thanks. He thought highly of you, Sheriff."

Alex noticed George had left the helicopter running and was climbing up to the engine cover, so he went over to talk to him. "Can you fly us to the ventilation shaft?"

"I'd like to help you, Alex, but there is something going on with the engine. Can you hear that ticking sound?"

Alex listened for a moment. "You're right. We'll find another way. Thanks for the ride."

Alex strolled over to Spencer. "I guess we're going four-wheeling." He looked at Bruce. "Are you coming with us?"

"No, my place is here. I have a lot of scared people counting on me, so I'll see you when you get back. Good luck, for all our sakes."

When Bruce hurried away, Alex and Okawna climbed up into the cab while Spencer climbed in behind the steering wheel. As they drove out of the parking lot past the helicopter, Alex saw George leaning over the open engine cowling.

***

VENTILATION TUNNEL:
Once they turned off the asphalt, Alex and Okawna were tossed around in the cab as Spencer drove over virgin terrain and through several small ditches. From a distance, they saw the shadowed entrance of the ventilation shaft, about two hundred feet up the steep side of the gray mountains. Below

it was a narrow pyramid of darker gray stone, but on either side, the vertical gray rock appeared to be smooth.

***

Twenty minutes later, Spencer parked at the base of the mountain and everyone climbed out. "We'll have to haul everything up to the entrance."

Alex did not want to be responsible for Spencer's life right now. "I think you should let me and Okawna do this."

"I'm in better shape than I look, Alex. Besides, do either of you have any experience with explosives?"

Alex exchanged knowing looks with Okawna. "As a matter of fact, we do. It would be a shame to come back and find the truck covered with boulders. I just think you should stay here with your truck, just in case you need to get it out of the way in a hurry."

"Just make sure you come back in one piece, okay?"

"We'll do our best."

Okawna climbed up into the bed of the truck and handed down a pick, a shovel, and a satchel filled with dynamite and blasting caps, and then held up a separate backpack. "What's in here, Spencer?"

"Flashlights, water, and a first aid kit."

Okawna handed it down to Alex and jumped out of the truck. "We'll see you soon."

"Hang on a minute."

Spencer climbed into the cab, grabbed a portable radio from the glove compartment, and held it out to Okawna. "I'll be listening in my truck, so keep me informed of what's going on."

Okawna clipped the radio onto his belt. "It won't work once we get inside, but at least I won't have to yell down at you from the entrance."

Okawna reached down and grabbed the satchel and pick, while Alex slipped the backpack over his shoulders and grabbed the shovel. "I'll call you when we get ready to set off the explosives."

Spencer leaned back against his truck and watched their ascent, and when they reached the top, he waved back at Okawna standing at the opening of the ventilation shaft. A second later, they disappeared inside the mountain.

***

The first fifty feet of the five-foot diameter tunnel were clear, but then the beam of Alex's flashlight revealed a lot of rubble and a few large rocks ahead. "These are recent."

Okawna aimed his flashlight at the ceiling. "I just hope this whole tunnel doesn't collapse when we set off the explosives."

Alex stopped walking. "We should see what Spencer gave us to work with."

Okawna opened the zipper on the satchel while Alex pointed his flashlight inside. "It's dynamite, all right. Six sticks with long detonation cords."

Alex studied the writing on the plastic tag attached to a timer actuator. "We only have a ten-minute delay. I hope it's enough time to get back to the entrance."

Okawna closed the satchel. "Onward."

After fifteen minutes of carefully memorizing the most hazardous areas for their return, the way was blocked by a gray concrete wall sealing the end of the tunnel. Okawna moved the beam of his flashlight around the outside edges, where the rock was fastened to the concrete. "The facility has to be on the other side, but without knowing how thick the wall is, it's hard to determine how much explosive to use."

Alex smirked at his friend. "Knowing the government and secret facilities, I'd say very thick. We only have one shot at this, so I say we use all of it and hope there is nobody on the other side."

Okawna studied the outside edges where the concrete extended past the end of the stone of the tunnel. "We're in luck. The earthquake created a gap between the rock and the concrete. We can use it like a shaped charge."

Alex held the actuator while Okawna inserted the sticks of dynamite in several locations around the gap. When he was finished, Alex slid the ends of the detonation cords into holes in the actuator. "All set. Ready when you are."

Okawna looked at his wristwatch. "Go."

Alex pressed the button and set the actuator on the ground. "Let's go."

Okawna did not even look at his watch until they stepped out of the tunnel. They moved to both sides of the opening, and Okawna keyed the portable radio. "Fire in the hole, Spencer."

Chapter 16

STILLWATER:

Arty could not remember a time when so many people had crowded into his restaurant. They all wanted information about the earthquakes, but he didn't know what to tell them. All conversations stopped when Rose turned up the volume on the radio.

"Yellowstone National Park is being evacuated, and we have an unconfirmed report there is a possibility of a major eruption."

Questions were yelled at Arty as if he had the answers. "I don't know any more than you do."

He was relieved when the bell on the door chimed and Bruce walked in. "Oh, thank goodness you're here, Sheriff. Everybody wants to know what's going on and I don't know what to tell them."

The room was suddenly quiet as everyone stared at him, so Bruce looked around at the familiar faces. "I know you're all scared, but we have to remain calm. There is a chance the earthquakes are going to continue for a while, and there is a possibility we could lose power. The best place for you to be is at home. Just make sure you have plenty of fresh water, and gather all your flashlights, batteries, portable radios, and any food you can find. I think if we all stay calm, we can get through this. Now please folks, why don't you all just head on home?"

"Is it true," a woman asked. "Yellowstone is going to erupt?"

"Who said anything about an eruption?"

"We just heard on the radio they are evacuating the park because of an eruption."

"As far as I know, it's just a precaution because of the seismic activity. Now, please. Just go home and be prepared to lose power."

Bruce walked over to the counter near Arty as everyone walked out the door. "How are you holding up, my friend?"

Arty chuckled softly. "There hasn't been this much excitement in this little town since Walter Raincloud came back with the Congressional Medal of Honor. So, what's our plan, Sheriff?"

Bruce wasn't sure how much he should tell him. "Alex thinks the earthquakes are being caused by something in the old mine."

"I just knew it was them roughnecks."

"He and Okawna are trying to get inside to stop it. If they can pull it off, this will be over. If not, there isn't really much we can do."

"I was thinking about closing the restaurant, but I know people will keep coming in wanting information. Especially those at the far end of the county. I'm sure these earthquakes are scaring the heck out of them."

"I'll keep you company until everyone leaves."

"Good. Let me pour you a cup of coffee."

Chapter 17

COBRA:

Rita, Henry, and Chris sat in silence, each lost in their own thoughts about what might happen to them when a huge concussion wave and a thunderous boom filled the lounge. They all flinched and bent over, covering their heads as the white acoustic tiles dropped from the ceiling, crashing onto their backs and arms.

When the tiles stopped falling, Henry reached over and grabbed Rita's arm. "The earthquakes are getting worse!"

Chris stood from his chair. "That was no earthquake. It was an explosion. Let's go see what happened."

When they stepped out from the lounge, they were engulfed in a cloud of gray dust as they carefully made their way across the floor. As the haze slowly cleared, they saw the device lying on the floor and covered in shattered pieces of gray concrete.

Rita looked up at the ceiling. "There's a hole in the roof. Something up there must have exploded. Maybe a storage area."

Chris studied the hole in the side of the dome. "That's a strange place to store explosives."

Henry felt his heart rate increase with a sense of hope. "Perhaps we can climb up to those rails and see if it is a way to get out."

Chris looked up at the overhead. "I can get close, but we could never make it from the rail to the opening. It's just too high."

Henry grabbed Chris's arm. "I do not want to stay in here! I must get out! Could you go up and make sure?"

"I can do that. Just step back in case any more debris falls down."

Henry let go. "Yes, of course. Thank you, my friend."

Chris walked across to a ladder mounted on the wall and started climbing. When he reached the top and stepped onto the rail, he used the one-inch steel rods supporting them from the ceiling for balance. Unfortunately, they were spaced six-feet apart. He had to let go of one to grab the next one and realized it would be difficult for Henry to navigate.

He continued until he was directly below the opening and stopped, but it was just as he thought. The four-foot hole was five feet above his outstretched arm, and he could never jump that high.

Henry shifted from foot to foot as he nervously watched Chris stop below the hole. "Is it a way out?"

Chris felt bad as he looked down at Henry. "It might be a short tunnel, but I don't see any light. We can't get into it anyway because it's beyond my reach. I'm sorry, Henry."

***

Alex and Okawna turned their faces away from the roiling cloud of dust spewing out from the tunnel. It took several minutes to dissipate so they could look inside, but the light from their flashlights could only illuminate ten feet further ahead.

Alex noticed the dust wasn't moving out of the tunnel. "We may not have blasted our way through. I don't see any air movement. Let's find out what happened."

Okawna brought up the radio. "We're going back inside, Spencer. See you in a few minutes."

***

Henry lowered his head in defeat, his brief sense of hope now shattered like the concrete on the floor. Rita noticed Henry's dejection and reached out to him, but he stared at her with a look, warning her to stay back. She tried to rationalize her reason for kidnapping him, but her actions seemed so sinister in retrospect. He had been little help, anyway.

Chris was carefully making his way back to the ladder when he caught a flash of light in his peripheral vision. He spun back around and looked up at the opening, where flashes of white light appeared to be bouncing around the interior. He cocked his ear toward the opening when he heard a quiet voice, but it stopped.

A few moments later, Chris heard a male voice say, it worked, and his heart rate increased as he yelled down at Rita and Henry. "I hear voices! Someone's coming. It must be a tunnel to the outside of the mountain."

Rita stared up at Chris. "Who is it?"

"I don't know. Maybe the guards found a way in."

A moment later, Henry heard a familiar voice and smiled. "It is Alex! He has found me! We are here, Alex! We are here!"

Alex was almost to the opening when he turned his head and grinned at Okawna. "I hear Henry."

He stepped to the edge and stared down at his friend's smiling face on the other side of the room. "Are you okay, Doc?"

Henry thought his heart would burst. "Oh, Alex. I am so glad to see you again."

"You need to turn off the device. It's creating a lot of problems."

"It is not the device, Alex. Whatever they were doing in this facility is causing the problems."

"I know. It's a meteor they brought back from the moon that's causing the earthquakes." He stared at Rita. "It's the frequencies you're using that activate it."

Rita looked up at Alex, but ignored his glaring eyes. "That last earthquake happened without our help. It did it on its own, so don't blame me."

Alex held his rage in check. "Right. Let's get you out of here, Doc."

Chris was standing below on the railing, listening, and stepped away enough to look up at Alex. "Do you have any rope?"

Alex looked down at the stranger. "No, and who are you?"

"I'm Chris, one of the guards."

"You're part of this kidnapping?"

Chris felt his face flush. "For my part, I am, and I'm sorry. I didn't know Henry before now."

"That's a poor excuse for a kidnapping."

Henry knew Chris was just doing his job. "He is a friend, Alex."

Alex was less than convinced. "Can you lift Henry up to me?"

Chris felt a sense of relief and gave Alex a grateful smile. "You bet I can."

Chris turned and worked his way back to the ladder and hollered down at Henry. "I'll meet you at the top."

Alex watched as Henry climbed the ladder, followed closely by Rita. Chris helped Henry keep his balance by grabbing the next rod and reaching back to take his hand to help him across, and then reached across for Rita. When they reached the area below the opening, Alex lay prone on the ground and reached down to grab Henry's hand.

Chris grabbed the nearest rod for balance and stooped slightly to extend his thigh. "Henry, I want you to grab my hand and climb onto my knee, and then step up onto my shoulders." He saw the hesitation in Henry's eyes. "Do you want to get out of here?"

Henry was desperate to get out of this bomb shelter, so steeled his nerves for the task and grabbed Chris's hand. He placed his other hand on Chris's shoulder as he stood on his knee, but could not tell if it was himself shaking or Chris. He continued up onto Chris's shoulders, using the young man's strong arm for balance. "Now what do I do?"

"Just hang on while I stand up, and you should be able to reach Alex when I do it. Here we go."

In one swift movement, Henry was hurled into the air. He reached up to grab Alex's hand and was instantly hauled up over the edge into the tunnel.

Henry rolled onto his back while he tried to stop shaking. "I am so glad to see you, Alex. Thank you for coming for me."

"You're welcome, Doc. Let me help you up so we can get out of the way. Okawna can help your friend get out."

"Yes, of course."

Once Henry and Alex moved past him, Okawna looked down from the opening at Chris. "How far up can you reach?"

Chris stood on his toes and reached up for the opening. "That's it."

Okawna lay prone and reached down. "You can make it if you jump, but you're going to have to trust me."

Chris looked down and realized if he missed, he'd fall and die and then looked up at Okawna. "What about Rita?"

Okawna glared down into the eyes of the familiar face. "What about her?"

Rita broke eye contact and quickly checked her footing and then grabbed the next rod and moved next to Chris to stare up at Okawna. "You can't just leave me!"

"Sure I can. You kidnapped my friend and almost got him killed, and that I cannot forgive. Chris? Are you ready?"

Chris hesitated. "I'm not sure how I feel about this."

"I don't see that you have much choice. You're welcome to stay where you are."

Alex moved back to the opening. "What's the holdup?"

Rita stared up at Alex. "He won't help me out of here!"

Alex stared at her for a moment. "You and your compatriot are going to be arrested for what you did to Henry."

"I know, and I'm sorry. I realize that now. I'll take my punishment, but just get me the hell out of here!"

"Where's the other device?"

"Preston just said he'll have it delivered here. Honest, Alex. I don't know."

Alex looked down at Okawna, who shook his head no. "I know how you feel, but I'd prefer not to have her death on my conscience right now."

Okawna sighed in frustration. "Okay, Chris. Hand her up."

Alex turned and noticed Henry hurrying along the tunnel, so quickly caught up with him. "Wait up, Doc. We should wait for the others."

"I cannot wait, Alex. I must get out of here!"

Alex glanced over his shoulder at Okawna, still reaching over the edge. The ground suddenly heaved up, tossing him and Henry off their feet onto the floor. When large rocks slammed down into the tunnel, he spun back around and saw the collapsing boulders hammering down on Okawna, still lying face down.

Alex turned around, searching through the roiling dust until he saw Henry lying on the ground under a small pile of rubble. Out of the corner of his eye, he saw Okawna's leg move, but he was torn between trying to save him and saving Henry.

He chose Okawna and dragged smaller rocks out of the way, and then hauled on one extremely large boulder, but it wouldn't budge. He grabbed Okawna's foot and pulled with all his strength, desperately trying to drag him back from the opening, only to slip and fall on the loose rocks. He scrambled to his feet and grabbed the leg again as more rock crashed down on Okawna's back, making it even harder.

The ground heaved up again, slamming him against the wall. Stars erupted in his vision as a searing pain raged in his head and he lost his balance, toppling backward onto piles of rock.

The shaking suddenly stopped, but when he looked back, the ceiling above Okawna had collapsed, burying him alive.

"NO!"

He beat his fist against a boulder, chastising himself for caring about Rita, realizing he should have left her to die! If he had ignored his conscience, Okawna would have made it! "DAMN YOU RITA!"

***

Chris stared up helplessly as the dome crashed down, driving him backward off the rail. He glimpsed Rita tumbling from the railing before his mind went blank. The last thing Rita saw as she fell through the air was Okawna's arm protruding from the ceiling before everything blinked out.

Chapter 18

STILLWATER:

Arty sighed with relief when the last person stepped out the door, but then the floor shook and the windows rattled. "I guess Alex didn't get it turned off."

The magnitude of the shaking increased as brass frame pictures jumped off the wall. The glass window exploded as the wooden structure was ripped apart, and then a section of the roof fell down, blocking the exit.

When the Sheriff grabbed his arm and tried to drag him across the debris, Arty jerked it free. "Rose!"

Arty ran into the kitchen and found her hunkered down against the freezer. "Time to go, sweetie." When she looked up at him, he helped her up from the floor. "Here we go, just watch your step."

Arty helped Rose across the debris, then guided her out through the shattered window. He slid his arm around her shoulder as they turned around to stare in numb shock at what was left of their restaurant, and then Arty looked over at Bruce. "What should we do, Sheriff?"

Bruce was at a loss for words. "I don't know what to tell you, my friend. I guess we need to find a place to hunker down until this is over."

"You said if Alex can do what he's trying to do, this will all be over, right?"

"I won't lie to you, Arty. I don't think he has a chance in hell of pulling it off. I'm still responsible for the people in this town, so I can't leave, but you might want to consider it."

"I'll tell you what I'm gonna do, Sheriff. I'm going to load my truck with whatever supplies I can find and get out of town."

"I think you're doing the right thing."

Deputy Arnold Wilson stopped his patrol car and jumped out, then studied the damage to the restaurant as he approached the Sheriff. "Why is this happening, Bruce?"

Bruce explained the situation to him. "Not really much we can do about it."

Arnold whistled softly and pointed to the wide crack in the parking lot. "This is gonna get bad, aint it, Sheriff?"

"I'm afraid so. I need you to drive around and check the extent of the damage." When Arnold hurried to his patrol car, Bruce turned to Arty. "You and Rose had better get going."

Bruce climbed into his patrol car and drove down to the municipal building. The main structure was still standing, but all the windows had shattered. He parked and leapt out of the patrol car, and then ran up the steps, already dreading what he would see when he got inside.

When he ran through the opening where the doors had been, he stopped when he saw the gray hair on the desk under the rubble. The wall behind Helen had collapsed, crushing her under a pile of concrete blocks. One hand protruded from the rubble, still clutching the telephone. He looked down both hallways, now blocked by debris, and realized there was nothing he could do, so he turned and left the building.

Chapter 19

VENTILATION SHAFT:

When the shaking subsided, Alex stood, but he could not see any sign of Okawna. He pulled on the massive boulders, but after several minutes when they wouldn't budge, he stopped trying. "I'm sorry, my friend."

"Alex? Are you there?"

Alex turned and looked down the tunnel through the dust and saw Henry on the ground, so he hurried back to help him up. "We'd better get out of here. Can you walk?"

Henry took Alex's hand and stood. "What happened to Okawna and the others?"

"It's just you and me now, Doc. We'd better hurry before we get trapped in here, too."

Alex looked around for the backpack with the supplies, but it was buried somewhere under the debris. Hopefully, Spencer had more water and first aid supplies in his truck.

The going was slow as Alex and Henry made their way over the recently fallen rocks and boulders to the entrance, but when Alex looked down, his heart sank. Sections of Spencer's truck protruded from beneath a pile of boulders.

He and Henry carefully made their way down through the debris, and once safely on the ground, Alex searched for any sign of Spencer, but didn't find any trace of him. He could only assume he was somewhere beneath the boulders.

He reached into his front pocket and brought out his cellphone and realized he didn't know the Sheriff's number. If he called the ranch to get it, he would have to tell them Okawna was killed during the rescue, which was something he would rather do in person. Suddenly, he remembered seeing George's telephone number on the side of the helicopter and punched in the numbers. After several rings, he finally answered.

* * *

THE THEATRE:

When his phone rang, George banged his head against the engine cowling, then rolled into a sitting position and dug it out of his pocket, but didn't recognize the number. "Who is this?"

"This is Alex Cave."

"Hey, we've just had a major earthquake. What happened? I thought you guys were going to shut it down."

"It can't be stopped, George, and it's going to get worse. Okawna and Spencer were killed during the rescue, and my friend and I are stuck out here below the ventilation shaft. Any chance you could come and get us?"

"I can't find the problem with the helicopter, so until I do, I'm grounded. I'll come and pick you up as soon as I can."

"Thanks, George. We'll be walking toward Stillwater."

* * *

THE MOUNTAIN:

Alex put away the phone and looked at Henry. "We have a long walk ahead of us, Doc. Are you up to it?"

"I am sorry about all this, Alex."

"It wasn't your fault. Let's get started."

"You have a nasty cut on the side of your head, Alex. Are you sure you are all right?"

Alex tried to ignore his throbbing headache. "I'm Okay." He turned and walked across the desert toward Stillwater, with Henry at his side.

Chapter 20

STILLWATER:

Bruce left the municipal building and climbed into his patrol car, but just sat for a moment and stared at the old building. He doubted even Patrick had enough money to rebuild it.

He drove out of the parking lot and took the first road headed south and then turned off the pavement onto a narrow dirt road and stopped next to a collapsed wooden shed. Straight ahead, his home was a pile of shattered memories, and except for his time away in the Marine Corps, he had lived in the house all his life. He thought about climbing out to scrounge through the rubble for pictures, but if what Alex had told him was coming true, it wouldn't matter. He reigned in his emotions, backed out onto the road, and headed back toward town.

***

Bruce drove through the rural section of town, where the streets were laid out in parallel and crossing roads, with one house on each block. Most of the houses were crumbled piles of colored wood and asphalt shingles, but Arty and Rose's old home behind the restaurant was still standing.

He drove his SUV to Arnold's house, which appeared to be leaning at an odd angle, but something else looked out of place, and when he was within ten feet, he realized what it was. He shoved the transmission into park and leapt out the door and then ran over to Arnold lying on the sidewalk. He knelt down to feel for a pulse on the neck and saw the side of his deputy's head was caved in.

When he noticed Arnold's revolver was gone, he jumped up to look around, placing his hand on the butt of his own pistol. He slowly turned in a circle, but did not see anyone, and then realized Arnold's patrol car was missing. He looked down at his friend one more time. "You were a good deputy. Thanks."

He climbed back into his patrol car and continued down the streets, recognizing the people from the restaurant returning to determine the damage to their homes. He received the occasional nod, but they already knew what to expect, so he did not stop. When he drove back onto the main street, nothing of the red brick buildings was left standing. He slowly drove around the debris, searching both sides of the street for anyone still alive.

He stepped on the brakes when he heard a gunshot, then two more. From the direction of the sound, they were coming from the parking lot in front of the municipal building. He drove as fast as possible around the debris, and then stopped when he saw two groups of people in the parking lot. They were armed with rifles and pistols, shouting at each other from twenty feet apart.

He pulled over so his vehicle was between the two groups and slowly climbed out, and now, they were all staring at him, and he wondered what would happen next. He studied the people in one group, and then did the same to the other, recognizing all of them, including the oldest one named James. "What's going on here?"

"It's Gary and Jennifer, Sheriff. We've been scrounging around for anything useful and they want to take it from us."

"That's not true," Jennifer hollered. "We were here first."

When James and Jennifer turned and glared at each other, he knew he had to do something. "I want all of you to calm down. We can all survive if we work together."

The two groups were suddenly looking past him, so Bruce spun around. It was the three Harrison brothers, all armed. "Oh, shit."

They were the town bad boys, and he had dealt with each one of them on several occasions, and knew this was going to get tricky, since the brothers only needed the slightest excuse to go on a rampage. The others were generally peaceful kids, and he realized his best course of action would be to confront the brothers.

He slowly approached the three Harrisons, careful not to bring his hand down near his revolver. "It seems we all have our problems today, boys. You're going to have enough trouble as it is. Let's just talk about this for a moment before somebody does something stupid."

One brother suddenly grinned, swung his shotgun up, and fired. Bruce leapt out of the way as a volley of gunfire erupted between the brothers and the mob. Bullets whizzed over his head as he lay on the ground, and then it was over.

Bruce glanced over at the brothers, where two were on the ground together, reeling in agony, but he could not see the third one. He turned and looked at the group of kids, and only two were still standing. Gary, who was cradling a bloody arm, and Jennifer, who was still pointing a shotgun in his direction.

He noticed the rage in her eyes as he slowly stood up and put his hand on the butt of his revolver. "It's over, Jennifer. Lower the shotgun."

"It was self-defense, Sheriff!"

"I know, but could you lower the shotgun?"

"The whole town's gone crazy!"

"Yes, it has. We can talk about it."

"No way. I'm leaving this nightmare."

A shot rang out and Jennifer flew backward onto the ground. Bruce turned and saw one brother sitting up while pointing a rifle at him. "Oh, damn!"

It felt like a hammer hit his left shoulder and spun him around. He lost his balance and slammed onto the asphalt and the back of his head erupted in pain, and he lay still for a moment, listening for any noise. The only sound was a soft moan, so he sat up to look around. The brother's bloody bodies were lying on the asphalt, and the kids were all lying on the stone steps.

He cringed as he put his hand against the hole in his left shoulder, grateful the bullet had passed through cleanly. He used his right arm to push himself off the ground and stood up and then placed his hand against the side of his patrol car to steady himself. He heard the moan again and looked at the steps, and it was Gary. He walked over and looked down at the young man, and the ragged red hole in the left side of his chest told him all he needed to know. The boy was not going to make it.

He suddenly realized the third and oldest brother, Kurt, would not hesitate to kill anyone in his way, and he might go for the helicopter to leave the area. He eased into his patrol car and raced out of the parking lot.

***

George was still on top of his helicopter, leaning over the engine, when he heard gunfire. He stood to figure out where it came from as two more shots rang out from some place in town and realized he was in big trouble. He closed the engine cowling and slid down off the helicopter. He jumped into the cockpit and flipped the switches to start the engine, but it would not turn over.

He jumped out of the cockpit, desperately trying to think of the reason the engines would not start, and then climbed on top again. With his head buried under the cowling, he discovered the problem. In his haste to get down, he had left one small cable unplugged. He was about to plug it back in when he heard footsteps below him. When he raised his head above the cowling, a young man with a shotgun was standing on the ground below him.

Kirk Harrison pointed a shotgun up at the man on the helicopter. "Fly me out of here!"

George stood up. "I can't. The engine won't start."

"You're lying. I saw you land earlier."

"I'm not lying. Why else would I be working on it?"

"Just get on down here and start this thing up or I'll blow a hole in your chest!"

George caught a flash of light out of the corner of his eye and looked over as the Sheriff's patrol car pulled into the parking lot. He looked down at the young man, now watching the sheriff.

Bruce pulled up next to the helicopter with his car only three feet from the boy. He slowly climbed out, closed the door, and casually walked around the front to lean back against the hood, eye level with Kurt. He did not want to provoke the situation, so was careful to keep his hand away from his revolver. "What the hell are you doing, Kurt?"

"I need a ride, Sheriff, and this guy is going to give me one."

"I don't want to kill you, son, but you know I will, so don't force my hand. I'll give you the chance to walk away right now, so be smart about this. You have enough problems to deal with. You don't want a problem with me."

To Kirt, the Sheriff's eyes seemed to bore right through him, and even though the officer was bleeding, he knew he would not win this fight. He slowly backed up, and then turned and ran across the parking lot, disappearing behind what was left of the theater.

Bruce sighed with relief and looked up at George. "How are you holding up?"

"I was getting a little worried, Sheriff. Alex is waiting for me to pick him up. He said they can't stop the earthquakes and things will get worse. He also told me Okawna and Spencer were killed during a rescue, but he managed to save his doctor friend."

Bruce took a long look around the area and his town was now in shambles, then he looked up at George. "I guess I'm done here for a while. I wouldn't mind going with you, but right now, I need someone to work on this shoulder. If you're up to it, I have a first aid kit in the car."

"I saw the blood on your uniform, but I didn't know it was yours. Let me see what I can do."

George got down and retrieved the kit from the patrol car, and then applied disinfectant and covered the entrance and exit wounds with pads and tape. "You'll want to take it easy and keep your left arm movements to a minimum, or it may start bleeding again."

"Thanks. I'll be all right."

"I found the problem with the engine. Give me a minute to finish working on it and we'll leave right away."

Bruce gently eased himself into the helicopter. "I think I'll just sit here for now."

Chapter 21

STILLWATER. THE DESERT:

When Alex noticed Henry stumble, he stopped at a dry streambed. "I could use a short break. How about you?"

"Yes, by all means." Henry eased himself down onto the sandy wall at the edge next to Alex. "I know how much Okawna meant to you, and I am deeply sorry for your loss."

"I know, Doc, and I'm sorry about your kidnapping. Why did Rita want the device?"

"I thought it was just greed, but she is in love with that Steve Preston fellow." Henry explained what he knew about the DAR Corporation and Preston's plans. "I will tell you this, Alex. I wish we had never located those devices."

Alex heard his phone ring and recognized the number. "I'm here, Jerry. What's going on?"

"The zipper effect is starting, Alex. Small eruptions are occurring around the perimeter of the magma pocket."

"How much time do we have before it blows?"

"At the rate these new eruptions are spreading, I'd say, within the hour."

"I've found the cause, but there is no way to stop it. Is there anything I can do to help you?"

"Everyone necessary has been notified, but there just isn't enough time to get organized. We estimate a five hundred mile blast radius, so even the people leaving the park may not get far enough away. Are you still in Stillwater?"

"I'm afraid so. I'm stuck out in the desert."

"You know that area will be demolished from the blast wave, so try to find some shelter."

"What about you? You are leaving, right?" The line was silent. "Jerry?"

"Good luck, Alex."

Alex looked down at the sand as he realized Jerry knew it was too late to save himself. "Yeah. You too."

Alex stood and reached down for Henry. "Time to go, Doc. Yellowstone is about to erupt."

Once they were moving across the desert again, Alex knew he needed to call the ranch. If the women leave right now, they would probably get far enough away. He dreaded having to tell them about Okawna over the phone, but he had no choice and entered the number.

***

OKAWNA RANCH:

After the last earthquake, Fala had convinced Judith it wasn't safe to stay inside the house, and they were sitting on chairs she had dragged down off the porch when the shaking had subsided. "Why don't you pack some clothes and stay with me until this is over?"

"I don't want to leave my home, Fala. Okawna said he and Alex would stop the earthquakes."

Fala knew Okawna had not told Judith the extent of what was happening, but she was hesitant to explain all the details. Should Alex and Okawna fail, perhaps the ranch would be far enough away from Yellowstone to escape the blast from an eruption. She noticed the tears forming in Judith's eyes, but knew there was not anything more she could say to ease her heartbreak.

She smiled when she saw Halona chasing a calico cat around the barn, but her smile slipped away when she thought about the possibility of Yellowstone erupting. For now, all she could do was hope Alex and Okawna stop it from happening.

Judith heard her phone ring and looked at the ID, but didn't recognize the number. "Hello?"

"Judith, this is Alex."

"Oh, Alex. We've just had a bad earthquake. I thought you and Okawna were going to stop them."

"I'm sorry, Judith, but it can't be done. Is Fala there?"

"Yes. She's right here."

"Put her on, please."

Fala saw the frightened look in Judith's eyes as she took the phone. "I'm here, Alex."

"Leave right this minute! Yellowstone is going to erupt, so don't pack anything, just head south as fast as possible."

"All right. Are you and Okawna going to meet us someplace?"

Alex hesitated. "Things are going to be very bad after the eruption, so keep heading south. Now get going, all right?"

"We'll leave immediately. Stay safe."

***

STILLWATER. THE DESERT:

Henry waited until Alex hung up. "Who was that?"

"Okawna's family."

"How far is it to Stillwater?"

"About ten miles."

"I wish I would have worn different shoes."

Alex didn't have the heart to tell him if the helicopter did not arrive soon, his shoes would not matter. As they continued across the desert, he kept thinking about Fala and Halona. Deep inside, he knew they could have been a family together, and now this happened.

Henry reached up and grabbed Alex's arm. "Do you hear that?"

Alex heard the deep thumping sound of an approaching helicopter and looked at his watch. Only fifteen minutes had passed since he had talked to Fala, and there might still be time to catch up with them on the road south. If he could get them into the helicopter, they could outrun the shock wave for sure.

A few moments later, Alex and Henry turned their faces away from the billowing sand as the helicopter set down. When the wind slowed, Alex followed Henry over to the open side door and helped him into the rear passenger seat next to Bruce and shut the side door. He climbed into the copilot's seat, buckled in, and put on the headset. "Thanks, George. Do you know the location of the Okawna ranch?"

"Yeah, it's east of here."

"Good. Yellowstone is about to erupt and I need to save his family, so head there as quick as possible,"

When the helicopter took off and headed east, Alex looked into the back seat at the bloodstained gauze around Bruce's shoulder. "What happened?"

"It's a long story, Alex. The entire town has been destroyed."

"I'm sorry my plan didn't work. Where are you headed?"

"We were hoping you could tell us."

"Listen, we can outrun the blast wave by going south, but I need to make sure the Okawna family is safe. They're heading south right now, so let's go pick them up on the way."

"You got it."

As they gained altitude, Alex stared out the window toward Yellowstone and saw small plumes of gray-brown ash climbed high into the air, forming a circle around the park. It was called the Zipper effect, and if one or two more small eruptions occur, thirteen hundred square miles of earth would be vaporized.

He turned forward and stared through the front window for Fala's car, and then he saw the red vehicle five miles away on a dirt road. Seconds passed by as if hours as the helicopter slowly closed the distance to the red SUV.

Alex realized if he could get her to stop, they would catch up much faster. He pulled out his phone and entered Judith's number, but it continued to ring. "Come on, answer!"

Bruce suddenly pointed north. "Oh my God! Look!"

Everyone turned and stared at the massive column of gas and ash rising high above the park. In the distance, the air appeared to be shimmering and moving in their direction, and George instinctively gained altitude as the shock wave of dust and sand rolled across the desert.

Alex spun back to the front window, helpless to save anyone in the SUV, and then he was suddenly hurled against the side door as the shock wave slammed into the helicopter. George regained control, and while the helicopter gained altitude, Alex stared down at the dust cloud rolling across the desert.

George brought the helicopter up to one-thousand-feet and hovered above the area where he had last seen the red SUV. Everyone stared out the windows, but the thick layer of dust hanging in the air made it difficult to see anything on the ground.

Bruce was the first to notice a splotch of red and pointed out the window. "I see it! It's right over there!"

George moved the helicopter over the area and the rotors blew the dust into a billowing cloud, churning away from what was left of the red SUV. The vegetation had been ripped from the ground and the wreckage lay strewn across the barren desert.

Even before the runners touched the ground, Alex threw open the door and leapt out, hitting the ground running. The main body of the SUV had collapsed into a ragged ball of twisted metal, but he hoped they could still be alive. He slid to a stop and every ounce of strength seemed to leave his body as he dropped to his knees.

Blood drenched black hair was draped across Fala's face, but it was only her head on the ground. Curly blond hair attached to a pink flap of flesh was trapped between two scissors of steel, and the legs of an older woman were no longer attached to a body.

Alex shook his fists at the sky. "NO! DAMN YOU RITA!"

Henry watched Alex slump down and slam his fists against the ground. He climbed out of the helicopter and ran over and then knelt beside him. "I am sorry, my friend, but there is nothing we can do for them, and we need to get moving."

Alex slowly stood and took one last look around. Watching his best friend die had been hard enough, but now, what could have been his new family lay in bloody pieces on the ground in front of him. He didn't know if he could take any more heartbreak today.

Henry gently grabbed his friend's hand. "It is not good for you to keep looking at them, Alex. Please come back to the helicopter with me."

George watched the two men shuffle over to him. When they were inside, he looked over at Alex. "Where to next?"

Alex wiped away a single tear and checked for a signal on his cellphone, but did not get one. "Can we make it to Salt Lake City, Utah? It's on the other side of the Rocky Mountains, so it should still be clear of the ash cloud."

George checked his fuel. "Barring a strong head wind, we should make it okay."

George continued to gain altitude as he pointed the helicopter west and headed across the desert. Their elevation increased over the mountains and they all stared north, where everyone but Alex found it hard to believe a volcano could cause such destruction.

The column of brown ash was hundreds of miles across and flowing in an easterly direction. On the western side of the Rockies, the ash had reached Pocatello, Idaho, but to the south, they could see that Salt Lake City had not yet been affected.

Twenty minutes later, the radio squawked, and they contacted the airport for landing instructions. George dropped his aircraft down on the tarmac a short distance from a news helicopter with people climbing inside, and then they all climbed out.

George left the group and hurried over to talk with a fellow pilot. "Where are you headed?"

"The station wants me to get shots of the eruption, so I'm taking one of our news people up to take a look."

"We just came from northwest Wyoming and barely made it out alive. The thermals are going crazy because of all the heat, so you'd better be careful up there. It's a wasteland as far south as Jackson Hole and east of Pocatello, Idaho, and the ash is drifting east past Casper, Wyoming, right now. I don't know what it's like north of the volcano, but if it's as bad as what I've seen so far, we're all in a lot of trouble."

While they waited for George to come back, Alex called Donner to arrange a flight to Nevada. "Has the ash reached the east coast yet?"

"No, but I've been informed of heavy accumulations across the northern plains, so it's only a matter of time. The President will be on Air Force One within the hour."

"What about you?"

"I need to coordinate the evacuation of our political leaders to NORAD."

"None of us can escape the eventual outcome, Martin."

"I know. Thanks for trying, Alex."

"Good luck."

Chapter 22

GROOM LAKE, NEVADA:

David Conway entered Hangar 5 and strolled over toward the spacecraft. The six-foot sphere was sitting on an inflatable donut-shaped rubber pad outside, with the reflection of his distorted face grinning back at him on the mirrored surface.

"I wonder what your purpose was on the spaceship."

The surface of the sphere shimmered as if turning into a liquid, and he took a step back. "Whoa!" He jumped back again when a small bald man suddenly stepped out. "Where did you come from?"

Paladin recognized the person with the shocked expression. "Hello, David."

It took a moment before David realized the person was wearing a silver jumpsuit, like the one Alex had found in the cargo hold. When he understood the magnitude of what it signified, his heart rate increased. He wasn't sure what to do except hold out his hand, but the man didn't accept it. "My name is David Conway."

"I know who you are. We've already met. I'm Paladin. Tell me what's going on right now."

David took a deep breath, trying to regain his composure. "Wow! You're one of the missing crew from the spaceship."

"No, I'm not. I'm a time traveler. Tell me what's happening on this planet right now."

"Well, I just found out Yellowstone erupted."

Paladin's shoulders sagged. "I told Alex it wouldn't work. Where is he?"

"He's just arrived from Salt Lake. How do you know Alex?"

"Take me to him."

"All right. Follow me."

David turned and headed for the door into the workspaces in the rear of the hangar. Once through the doorway, they continued down a hall past some spectators staring at a hairless man with no ear cartilages.

***

Alex was sitting at a table in the break room, staring into his coffee cup while replaying everything over in his mind, trying to think of what he could have done differently. Deep down, he knew it was just a way to stop thinking about all he had lost. Okawna had always had his back, but now he had let him down. Hell, he had let everyone down.

A vision of Fala and Halona sitting with him on the porch at the Okawna ranch was ripping at his heart. Should he have left Henry in the facility to begin with? He suddenly remembered the ultimate question that could never be answered. What if?

Alex looked up when David walked in, accompanied by a slim man in a familiar silver jumpsuit, and then he stood from the table. "Who's your new friend?"

"This is Mister Paladin. He just stepped out of the sphere."

"Hello again, Alex. It's just Paladin. What happened this time?"

Alex's eyebrow rose slightly. "This time? I'm not following you."

"The sphere is a time machine, and I've sent you back twice to stop the eruption. I told you it would not work."

Alex was speechless for a moment. "All right. Have a chair and start at the beginning."

Paladin waited until Alex and David were seated before joining them. "Do you remember the first time you touched the sphere?"

"Yes, when we found the spaceship."

"When you placed both hands on the surface, a small electrical field generated by your body activated a signal, and I was sent back through time to find out what type of life form it was."

David leaned forward and placed his arms on the table. "Where did you come from? Time travel? I didn't think it was possible. Do the rest of your people travel through time?"

Paladin glared at David in frustration and then looked across at Alex. "I'm growing tired of explaining this each time you fail. What happened this time? Did you remember what you needed to do?"

Alex was silent, pondering the fact he had traveled back in time. Twice. "I remember the electrical shock, but nothing else."

"You sprained your wrist the last time you tried to change the past. Tell me what went wrong this time."

Alex jumped up and leaned across the table, glaring at Paladin. "What do you mean, what went wrong? My best friend is dead and everyone on this planet are about to be wiped out! Everything went wrong! Are you saying I could have stopped this from happening?"

Paladin's stare didn't waver as he waited for Alex to settle down. "I tried to warn you. Do you remember what I told you about cause and effect?"

Alex sighed in frustration and plopped down onto the chair. "Of course not. I don't even remember meeting you."

"You mean well, but there are too many variables in time travel."

"If there's even a small chance I can stop this before it happens, then I'll just have to try it again."

"By trying to change so many events in the past, you create a cascade of events on an escalating scale. Each time you go back, you make things worse. How many times do you want to put yourself through all this anguish, Alex?"

"As many times as it takes. There has to be a way!"

"There is. I've told you twice, but you never remember what to do."

"And what's that?"

"You need only change one thing, Alex. When you locate the spaceship, stop Rita from calling her people and giving them your location. If you do that one thing, it will interrupt the chain of events that cause the volcano to erupt. The problem is you never remember what you need to do."

"There has to be a way for me to remember. There has to be!"

David suddenly remembered a conversation with Henry and got Paladin's attention. "If you can travel back in time, how come you didn't go back and change what happened to this planet one hundred and eighty million years ago? Your race would not have left this planet."

"Interesting question, but I am not from this planet. We have only recently acquired the technology and discovered the problem with time travel is the further back you need to go, the harder it is to arrive accurately at the exact time and place to make a difference. I could not change what happened to this planet that long ago, but I could save your species now. That is the only reason I allowed Alex to go back. If I help him change what happens this soon after the event, he can make a difference."

Alex leaned forward. "I'll try it again. I just need a way to help me remember what to do."

"I've already explained that each time you try, you only make matters worse. Have you looked in the mirror, Alex? The last time you tried, it was only your wrist that was injured. This time, you suffered a head injury. What will happen if you try it again?"

"I don't care. If I succeed, I won't have any injury."

"What if you die the next time?"

Alex leaned back and crossed his arms. "Then it won't matter. The eruption will happen just like right now, and everyone dies anyway."

David sat up straight. "Hold on a second, Alex. I don't want to die, and neither do the other billions of people on this planet. If there's a chance, you have to try. What if I go back this time instead of you? Maybe I'll remember what to do."

"No, it has to be me. This time, I remembered something felt wrong after I touched the sphere. I knew I was supposed to do something important, but I couldn't quite grasp what it was. Only that my feeling for Rita suddenly changed. Perhaps this next time I'll remember what to do."

Paladin was silent for a moment. "I would like to see your species of humans continue to evolve. If life on this planet is forced to begin again, the outcome may be completely different, and the DNA experiments of its previous inhabitants may not survive to become you."

"Yeah, and the dinosaurs will be the dominate species," said David.

Alex stood. "Then it's settled. Let's go to the sphere and send me back."

David had an idea and looked up at Alex. "What if we tattoo the information on your arm? That way, you'll know exactly what you need to do. That should work, right?"

Paladin shook his head no. "That's the paradox, David. If Alex succeeds, he will not have to go back in time in the first place, so he will not get tattooed."

Alex thought about his experience with the sphere. "I disagree. I felt the pain in my wrist this time. How could I feel the pain if I hadn't already hurt my wrist? If I get a tattoo right now and go back, it should still hurt when I come out. The difference will be I'll see it in black letters. That should work."

Paladin stared up at Alex. "Do you know the exact instant when Rita called her accomplice? When you go back, it will all start over again when you touch the sphere, and it may already be too late to stop her from making the call."

Alex slumped back down into the chair. "You're right. I don't know exactly. Wait a minute. I gave her a ride back to the island after I dropped Okawna off on the Mystic. Cellphones don't work that far out to sea, so she must have taken the satellite phone from the bridge. That's how I can stop her from making the call. I'll take the phone away from her when she tries to get a ride back to the island."

David realized something. "We still have a problem, Alex. I doubt anyone here has a tattoo machine."

"Use a scalpel to cut the message into my arm."

David's jaw dropped open. "Are you crazy?"

"I suppose I am, but it's the only way to make sure I get the message."

"Do you realize how many cuts it would take to explain everything?"

"Then we'll just have to keep it short. I'll just have it read, stop Rita."

Paladin was skeptical. "It's a very vague message. Will it be enough information? Will you know exactly what you need to do?"

"This last time, I suspected Rita was up to something, so I'll know what it means."

"All right. Just remember, if it doesn't work, you could escalate the problem. You may die this time."

Alex stood again. "I'll take the risk. Like I said before. What have I got to lose?"

David gave a short laugh as he stood. "Only the entire human race, Alex."

Alex suddenly felt uneasy. Everyone was counting on him again, only adding to the weight on his shoulders.

Paladin got up. "I'll meet you at the sphere. I'm always surprised when no one here seems to care that I'm different from everyone else."

David grinned. "You should see some of the people outside this base. Believe me, some of them look more alien than you do."

When David and Paladin headed back into the hangar, Alex continued down the hall and out of the building. He imagined the look he was about to get from a surgeon and grinned.

***

Alex entered the infirmary, where a young female nurse listened to his request. When her expression was just what he had imagined, he smiled.

Tammy Baker stared at the famous Alex Cave. "You're joking, right?"

"I wish I was. It's important."

"If you say so, but no doctor is going to do it. It will have to be me. Take off your shirt and have a seat."

Tammy turned to grab what she needed from a drawer. "Rumor has it Yellowstone erupted a little while ago."

"That's right."

She sat on a stool and sterilized the area on Alex's left forearm. "My friend said it won't take long to kill everything on the surface. Is that true?"

"Why are you asking me?"

"Everybody knows who you are, Mister Cave. You're a legend around here."

Alex shifted his position in the chair, uneasy with the compliment. "Legend's a strong word. Why would anyone think that?"

"You're going to feel a few stings when I numb the area. Well, you discovered the crystals and stopped Menno Simons from taking the entire world's oil, and you stopped us from a new ice age last week. If that isn't a legend, what is?"

Alex squirmed in his seat, but not from the stings. "It was just luck."

"My friend heard you talking in the cafeteria. He said you have a plan to stop this eruption."

Alex's posture stiffened, chastising himself for talking in a public area, since the last thing he needed right now was more people counting in him to fix this. "Just start cutting, all right?"

"Okay. You just want me to carve STOP RITA on your arm? That's all you want it to say?"

"That's right."

"How fancy do you want the letters?"

"I don't care, as long as I get the message."

Tammy grinned. "Okay. Here we go."

Alex stared into space while she cut into his arm. A few minutes later, he stood and checked the bandage covering the cuts. "Thanks."

Tammy noticed the other scars on Alex's body as he put on his long-sleeved shirt. "Good luck, Mister Cave. We're all counting on you."

Alex sighed in frustration. As he hurried out of the room, he wondered how he seems to always get himself into these situations."

***

When Alex strode into the hangar, David and Paladin were standing next to the sphere, so he went across to join them. "That looks familiar. I guess they didn't have a problem getting it out of the spacecraft."

David checked out Alex's body, noticing the bulge under his left shirtsleeve. "How did it go?"

"I'm ready. Okay, how does this thing work?"

Paladin indicated for Alex to stand close to the sphere. "I'm going inside to set the controls. When the surface stops shimmering, place both hands on the side of the sphere. It will be instantaneous and you shouldn't feel a thing. Are you ready?"

Alex looked at David. "I guess I'll see you again in a moment."

David reached out and gave Alex a hug. "Good luck."

Alex stepped back and looked at Paladin. "Let's do this."

When Paladin placed his hand on the sphere, Alex's jaw dropped slightly when he appeared to slip through the surface. A second later, the outside of the sphere looked like swirling tides of mercury for a second. When he saw his reflection, he placed both his hands on the surface and vanished.

Chapter 23

ALASKA. A TINY ISLAND IN THE ALEUTIAN CHAIN:

"Damn!" For a fraction of a second, Alex's left forearm felt as though it had been sliced open, but the pain went away. He looked over the top of a large silver sphere at his best friend, who looked puzzled.

Okawna stared at Alex. "Are you all right?"

Alex looked around the inside of the cargo hold with a sense of Déjà vu. He had a strange sensation there was something very important he needed to do, but it was just on the fringe of his memory, like a dark cloud in the recesses of his mind. "What just happened?"

Okawna thought it an odd question. "You touched this thing and swore in pain. Don't you remember?"

"Not really, but it all seems familiar. Let's go back to the beach so I can call Donner with the good news."

Once back outside, Alex entered Donner's private number. "We did it, Martin, but we need some support. I'm sure we're not the only ones who know about this island."

"I already have the Coast Guard on standby, so I'll call them right away."

"What about military support?"

"That will take a little more time, but I'll make the call. The Coast Guard should arrive within the hour. Is Okawna with you right now?"

"Yes."

"Tell him to call home. His father had a fatal heart attack."

Alex realized he already knew Donner was going to say that same thing. "Oh. All right. Thanks."

Alex handed the phone to Okawna. "Your family needs to get in touch with you right away."

While Okawna made his call, Alex stared at the spacecraft while thinking about recent events. They had accomplished the mission by shutting down the devices, so why did it feel like he wasn't finished?

Okawna hung up and looked at Alex. "Listen, I need to get home, but I don't want to leave you with no backup."

"Rita can handle herself, and I have David, Mike, and Joshua to help. Let's get back to the Mystic so the helicopter can take you to the airport in Seward."

Okawna hesitated. "That's not much help."

"Donner said the Coast Guard should be here soon, so I'll be okay. Let's go."

Alex and Okawna climbed into the motorboat, and Okawna shoved them away from the dock. Alex sat behind the steering wheel and drove back to the Mystic.

***

Rita was standing behind the doors out onto the stern, watching the motorboat heading toward the ship. She glanced back to make sure no one was around and then slid her pistol from her coat pocket. She tucked it behind her belt at her back, pulled her coat over it, and then strolled out onto the deck. When the boat bumped against the stern, she jumped in. "Can I get a ride back?"

Alex looked at Okawna, who climbed out. "I'll be back in a minute."

Alex shoved off from the stern, started the engine, and drove across to the island. A few moments later, the boat stopped against the dock and Rita stepped out and smiled. He was about to drive back to the Mystic, but had a strong desire to stay, as if a haze in his mind was clearing.

Rita noticed Alex's hesitation. "Is something wrong?"

"Maybe I should go with you."

Crap! Rita thought. "Don't be silly, I'll be fine. Go say goodbye to Okawna before he leaves."

"Maybe you're right."

Rita knew better than to let Alex get suspicious, so she turned and headed toward the steps up to the crater. When she reached the V, she was tempted to look back, but resisted and headed down the other side.

Alex stared after Rita as she disappeared over the edge of the crater. For some odd reason, he suddenly hated her, as if she had done something terrible to him. He thought it was just too crazy an idea, since they had been so intimate, so let it drop.

When he reached down to shove off from the dock, he suddenly remembered the pain in his left forearm and straightened up. When he rolled up his sleeve, his eyebrow went up when he saw someone had used lightning bolts as letters to spell STOP RITA.

He shut off the engine and stepped onto the dock, tying the bow rope to the cleat as he stood. The looming black cloud in the back of his mind was slowly clearing as he climbed over the ridge of the crater. When he saw Rita hurrying across the beach, an incredible sense of rage was nearly overpowering. He didn't understand why, but knew he had to stop her from doing something.

When Rita heard someone running across the gravel, she had a gut wrenching feeling it was Alex. "Damn, I hate that guy!"

When the footsteps stopped, she turned around, ready to smile and act innocent. She wasn't afraid of much, but the venomous look in his eyes seemed to bore right into her brain. "What's wrong with you, Alex?"

It took every ounce of his self-control to keep from knocking her to the ground. After a few deep breaths, he let his shoulders relax. "I'm not sure what's going on right now, but I'm taking you back to the Mystic."

Rita tried to relax, wondering if he was onto her plan. He was being very vague, and seemed to have a hard time remembering something. "You're scaring me, Alex. What's wrong with you?"

"I said, let's go!"

When she hesitated, he felt like grabbing her arm and dragging her back to the motorboat. "Now, Rita!"

She knew Alex meant it, but he couldn't prove anything, and now was not the time to argue. "All right, already."

Alex followed Rita back to the motorboat. They stepped in and he indicated for her to sit in the seat next to him, and then took her across to the Mystic.

***

Okawna was waiting for the motorboat on the stern, wondering why Rita was coming back as he caught the bow rope and tied it to a cleat. "What's up, Alex?"

When Alex grabbed her arm, Rita felt her heart rate increase, wondering how much Alex knew. "What's your problem?"

"Just get out of the boat."

Rita didn't like where this was leading, but stepped out onto the deck and waited until Alex climbed out. "Would you mind telling me what this is about?"

Alex had a strange intuition. "Empty your pockets."

Rita brought the satellite phone out from her coat pocket, careful not to expose the pistol tucked into the rear of her pants. "That's it."

When Alex saw the phone, he felt an adrenalin rush. "I'll take that."

She held it out to him. "I was just taking it over to Henry. He said he needed to make a call."

"I'll take care of it."

When Alex took the phone, it felt as if the weight of the world had been lifted off his shoulders, but he didn't understand why. Only that his nagging feeling was gone.

Okawna didn't know what to say, but trusted Alex to tell him later. "Do you want me to stick around?"

Alex hesitated. "Uh, no, I think everything is okay. Go home to your family."

Rita realized her plan was thwarted and turned to face Okawna. "You're flying back to the mainland? I'll go with you. I need to get off the water for a while, anyway. Just let me get my bag."

When Rita hurried across the deck, Okawna stared at Alex. "Would you mind telling me what that was about?"

Alex stared after Rita. "I have no idea. It was just a weird feeling something was wrong."

***

Rita threw her belongings into the tote bag, and then buried the pistol just under the surface of her clothes before zipping it shut. She knew Preston had a submarine capable of retrieving the device, and she knew the GPS location. If she could get ahold of Steve in time, he could salvage the device here in the Bering Sea. Now all she needed to do was get off this ship before Alex changed his mind.

***

Okawna noticed Alex staring across the water, lost in thought. "Are you sure you're all right?"

Alex turned to his friend. "I have all these images flashing through my mind. Things that could not possibly happen, but they seem so real." He rolled up his left sleeve. "Look at this."

Okawna stepped closer and read the letters formed by the red scar tissue before looking up and giving Alex a questioning stare. "Stop Rita? What does it mean?"

"I have no idea, but I think it had something to do with the phone"

When Rita stepped out onto the stern, she smiled and tried her best to look casual until she saw the strange look in Alex's eyes. She turned and grabbed the door handle on the side of the helicopter to get in.

Alex quickly moved over to stop her. "Hold on a second. What are you up to?"

She turned and smiled. "What do you mean?"

"Are you working with someone other than us?"

Rita shifted her weight, crossed her arms, and stared at Alex. "I don't know what kind of game you're playing, but I have done nothing wrong."

Alex realized she was right and just stared at her. He couldn't shake the feeling she was up to something and stepped closer to whisper in her ear. "I don't know what you're up to, but I'll be watching you."

When he stepped back, he saw the fear in her eyes and knew his suspicion was correct. Now she was leaving, so why didn't he feel relieved?

Rita looked away and climbed into the helicopter. She sat next to Lisa and looked over at Joshua lying on the opposite seat. All she had to do now was keep Okawna from asking too many questions and she would be free to continue her project.

Okawna gave Alex a hug. "Listen, we're going to have a memorial service for my dad next Saturday, and I wondered if you would come to my ranch. You've never been there, and I'd really like for you to meet my mom."

Alex didn't hesitate. "Of course I will. Just let me know what time."

"Great. I'll introduce you to my cousin, Fala."

Alex's shoulders slumped. "Don't do this to me again, Okawna. You know I'm not ready for another relationship."

"You don't have to marry her, Alex. I think you two might get along."

"You'd better get going. I'll see you in a week."

Alex watched his friend turn and climb into the helicopter, and as the rotors spun, he hurried up the stairs to the bridge. Once he was inside out of the downdraft, Bett took the helicopter into the air, and he sat down to watch it soar away across the water.

He stared at the island through the window, and could not stop thinking about the cuts on his arm. It was apparent the carver had talent, but when did it happen? Was he unconscious or awake? Why would he allow it in the first place?

When he heard the deep thumping of an approaching helicopter, Alex grabbed the binoculars off the console and trained them toward the sound. A moment later, an orange and white Coast Guard helicopter swung around the island and hovered over the stern deck, and then he heard a voice from the radio speaker.

"Mystic, this is Coast Guard Rescue Three at your service. I'd like to speak with Mister Alex Cave."

Alex grabbed the microphone. "This is Alex. It's good to see you."

"I'd like permission to lower a few Marines down to help you."

"Permission granted. What are your orders?"

"We'll remain here on standby until the jets arrive, but then we're to take you to the airport on Adak by order of Director Donner."

"I understand. Thanks for the assist."

Alex replaced the microphone as four soldiers slid down a rope onto the stern deck. He grabbed a portable radio and hurried down the stairs to greet them, and one man held out his hand.

"I'm Lieutenant Jackson, Mister Cave. What would you like us to do?"

Alex shook his hand. "Just Alex, will do, Lieutenant. Thanks for the help. I'll take two of you over to the island, and the other two stay here in case we get company."

The Lieutenant looked at his people. "Haskell and Vanzetti, stay here. Garcia, you're with me."

Mike was watching from behind the bridge and went down the stairs onto the stern and over to the group. "I see mister Donner came through for us."

Alex introduced Haskell and Vanzetti to Mike. "These men will stay here while I take the lieutenant and Private Garcia to the island."

Mike grinned at the Marines. "I'll be standing by."

***

When the motorboat slid against the dock, Alex shut off the engine and climbed out to tie it off to a cleat. He led the Marines up the steps to the V, but when he reached the rim of the crater, he waited for Jackson and Garcia to catch up so he could watch their expressions when they saw the spaceship. He wasn't disappointed when both their mouths opened slightly. "Wait until you see the inside. By the way, you cannot discuss anything you see on this island with anyone.

Ever. By order of the Director of National Security. Do you understand?"

Both men spoke together. "Yes, Sir."

Alex led them across the rusted ship and gangway, and continued across the gravel and stepped into the control room, where David and Henry were leaning over a console. "The Marines are here."

Henry looked up. "Sorry, Alex. I did not see you. Ah, you have brought company."

"This is Lieutenant Jackson and Corporal Garcia. They'll be watching over you when I leave. Donner wants to debrief me in D.C., so I'll be leaving once the jets get here."

"Contact Lewis as soon as possible. Tell him David and I need three new crystals if we are to fly this ship to Nevada."

"I will. Why don't you show our new friends around? I'll be back in a minute."

Alex's thoughts kept returning to the enigma of his scars, and the only connection was the sphere. He returned to the cave and followed the side of the spacecraft down to the eight foot airlock doors into the cargo area, and then walked straight over to the silver jumpsuit.

The mummified face staring up at him had all but turned to dust, barely recognizable as human. He knelt down to touch the silver suit, which didn't show any signs of deterioration, and the material felt like fine silk.

He didn't see any zipper or flap and wondered how this person had gotten inside. When he pulled up on the suit to roll it over, the remains passed right through the material. He stood and held it up by the shoulders, then looked down at the dust on the floor. Whoever it was, they wore the same size clothing as he did.

He let it drop and went over to the sphere. "What's your purpose on this ship?"

He remembered the scars on his arm had only hurt when he touched it, and wondered if it would hurt again. He slowly eased his palms toward the surface, hesitated, and then placed them against the sphere. When nothing happened, he stepped back and grinned.

His grin slipped away when the roar of a jet aircraft rumbled from the cave entrance. He turned and headed for the exit, snatching the suit from the floor and rolling it up before tucking it under his arm. He climbed out of the airlock into the cave, and then followed the mirror wall to the opening.

When he stepped outside the entrance, his friends and the marines were standing outside the spaceship, staring up at the sky, so he strolled across the beach to join them. "That sounds like my cue to leave."

David noticed the silver suit. "Where did you get the new clothes?"

"I think it belonged to one of the crew. I'll take it back and have it analyzed."

He heard the Coast Guard helicopter move into position over the Mystic. "I'd better get going. Call me if you need anything."

After hugs and fond farewells, Alex drove the motorboat back to the Mystic. He said goodbye to Mike before he was hauled up into the Coast Guard helicopter, and a moment later, he was heading to the Naval Air Station on Adak Island for a ride to Washington, D.C.

***

SEWARD, ALASKA:

As they approached the airport, Okawna realized Rita hadn't said a word to either him, Bett, Lisa, or Josh. Whatever Alex had said to her, she seemed subdued. He couldn't help wondering about Alex's scar message, and where it came from. Just when he thought this mission couldn't get any stranger, Alex threw another curve ball into the situation.

Once they set down on the tarmac, Rita grabbed her bag and said a quick thanks and goodbye to the group before hurrying across the concrete to the air terminal.

She hurried inside to ladies' restroom, and after making sure she was alone, she took out her cellphone and entered Preston's private number. "I'm in Seward. Things didn't go as we planned and we don't have much time, so listen carefully. I have the location of the device in the Bering Sea, but you need to get your water plane with the submarine here as fast as possible. It won't be long until Cave calls for a salvage operation to get the device out of the water. Here is the GPS location."

"What about you?"

"Send a private jet to pick me up here in Seward, and I'll fly to Wyoming and start getting everything ready at the COBRA facility."

"My jet will arrive in Seward in three hours. Once we recover the device, I'll bring it to you myself."

"Thanks. I'll see you at COBRA. I love you."

Rita heard a click from her phone. "Steve?"

She frowned and stared at the screen and saw the call was no longer connected. She figured it had to be the reception, so put the phone away and checked her face in the mirror.

Chapter 24

WASHINGTON, DC:

Martin Donner stood from behind his desk when Alex strolled through the doorway. They shook hands, and he indicated the chair on the other side of his desk. "Have a seat, Alex. Great job, by the way."

"Thanks, Martin." Alex explained everything. "I'm worried about Rita Harrow. I caught her trying to use the sat phone from the Mystic, and when I confronted her, she was in a hurry to leave the island. She's up to something, and I was hoping you could check her background for me?"

"Sure. Anything in particular you want to know?"

"Nothing specific. It's just a hunch."

"All right. The destroyer is on station near the island now, so everything is secure."

"Do they know what they're protecting?"

"No, the recovery operation is being coordinated from Adak on a need to know basis. Mister Norton is in route with the three crystals you requested." He grinned and shook his head. "It's hard to believe it still works after millions of years in a volcano."

"I think you should start the recovery of the device in the Bering Sea as soon as possible."

"The Navy has a ship in route as we speak. They should arrive tomorrow afternoon, Pacific time." Donner noticed the concern in Alex's eyes. "Is there something else?"

"Something happened to me when I touched a large silver sphere on board the spaceship, and then this suddenly appeared on my arm." He rolled up his shirtsleeve.

"Good grief! And you have no idea how it happened?"

"I don't have a clue."

"You should have it examined for any trace residue under the skin."

"I'll stop by the clinic once we're through here."

"What's in the bag?"

Alex brought out the silver suit. "One of the crew on the spaceship was wearing this. It has some interesting properties, and I'd like to send it to Nevada for testing."

"I'll make the arrangements. So, what's next for you?"

"I'm going to Okawna's ranch in Wyoming for his father's funeral on Saturday."

"Give him my condolences."

Alex stood. "I will. Keep me informed on the progress with the spaceship."

Donner stood to shake Alex's hand. "If I find out anything about Rita, I'll call."

"Thanks."

Chapter 25

FRIDAY. STILLWATER, WYOMING:
It was nearly 6:00 PM when Alex drove under the sign for the Okawna Land and Cattle Company. It had been a pleasant drive south on the eastern side of Yellowstone, though he was still dreading his meeting with Okawna's cousin. He would be polite, indulge in the general chitchat, and pretend not to be bored.

He parked near the house next to a red SUV and shut off the engine. A moment later, a small girl with wavy blond hair ran over and stared up at him through the open window.

"Are you the caveman?"

He laughed as he slowly opened his door and stepped out. "I suppose I am. What's your name?"

"Halona. Uncle Okawna saw you coming up the road and told me to bring you up on the porch."

When she held out her hand, Alex hesitated to accept it, wondering what Okawna was up to this time. He figured his friend must be softening the blow for meeting his ugly cousin. When he took Halona's hand, he was surprised when it felt oddly familiar.

Halona led him around the house, while asking questions about where he was from, where he worked, and why his name was cave man. "It isn't caveman. It's Alex Cave."

Halona giggled. "Uncle Okawna is funny, just like Uncle Richard. He's up in the sky with the white buffalo now."

Alex found it odd she would use a Native American Indian Philosophy. "That's nice."

When they walked around the corner, he saw three people sitting in chairs on the porch. Okawna, an older blond woman who he assumed was Okawna's mother, and an attractive woman with long black hair.

When he and Halona walked up the steps, all three gave him a puzzling stare. He quickly let go of Halona's hand, thinking he might be doing something improper, though he felt he hadn't.

Halona ran up the steps, laughing. "His real name is Alex Cave, Uncle Okawna."

When the three of them smiled, Alex relaxed as he climbed the steps. "Hello."

Okawna stood and gave his friend a hug. "Glad you could make it. This is my mom, Judith."

Alex stepped forward and reached down to shake her hand. "It's nice to meet you, and I'm sorry for your loss."

Okawna indicated the black-haired woman. "This is my cousin, Fala."

The woman stood and smiled, so Alex held out his hand. "Hello."

Fala accepted and then stopped smiling. "You'll have to excuse me, but have we met before?"

Alex had a feeling they had, although he knew they had not. "I'm sure I would have remembered."

"My mistake. I was surprised my daughter took to you so quickly. She's usually shy around strangers."

Now that she mentioned it, Alex realized he felt unusually comfortable meeting Fala for the first time. "I just thought she had a friendly personality."

Judith stood. "Have you eaten yet, Alex? I have plenty of leftovers."

"Actually, I haven't eaten since breakfast. That would be great."

"Have a seat and I'll bring it out for you."

When Alex sat down, Halona suddenly sat down beside him, smiling. He glanced over at Fala, who was grinning at his uneasiness. "I'm not used to being around young children. I'm more used to college students."

"Okawna told me you're a geology instructor in Bozeman."

"Geophysics, actually."

When Judith returned with a plate of food, Halona jumped down to chase a calico cat, so the four of them talked while Alex ate. When they talked about Okawna's father, Alex noticed Judith's faraway look.

Alex stood to take his plate into the house. "That was wonderful, Judith. Thank you."

Fala stood. "I'll take it in for you,"

"All right. Thanks."

Okawna noticed Alex staring after Fala. "I thought you two might hit it off."

"Yes, she's a very nice lady."

Alex grinned and stared out across the desert as the sun was dipping over the mountains. For some strange reason, he felt a sensation of familiarity with Fala, and he hadn't felt this way with any other woman but Sevi.

Alex turned when he heard the screened door open and smiled when Fala stepped out onto the porch. When she smiled in return, he wished he could sit with her for the rest of the evening, instead of driving to the motel in Stillwater.

Judith noticed how Alex and Fala looked at each other and smiled to herself. From what Okawna had told her about Alex, he was a good man. Fala had been through so much pain with her bastard ex-husband, she had hoped Fala and Alex would enjoy each other's company. She noticed Alex checking his wristwatch. "Why don't you stay here with us tonight, Alex?"

Alex was caught by surprise. "Oh, ah. I don't want to impose."

"Nonsense. You can sleep on the fold-out bed in the den."

"All right. I guess I'd better call the motel and cancel my reservation."

Fala was thinking she wouldn't see Alex again until the service tomorrow, sand was pleased he would stay here at the ranch. "I'll take care of it, Alex. My parents own the motel."

When Alex felt small fingers curl around his hand, he looked down at Halona's grinning, dirt-smudged face. She reminded him of his niece in Washington, and he smiled. He realized he had missed so much enjoyment by not being around her when she was that young.

The idea of having his own family someday had been his and Sevi's dream, but ever since he had lost her, he had given up on the idea. Perhaps Okawna is right, and it was time to get on with his life. He would just have to wait and see how things develop with Fala.

Halona stared up at Alex and pulled on his hand. "My mom says we have to sit down and be still to watch the sunset. You can sit next to me, Alex."

When he looked over at Fala, her lips formed a soft smile. "I think your mom is right. Where should we sit?"

***

SATURDAY AFTERNOON:

The ceremony had been nice, and now that the visitors had left, Alex was sitting on the grass under a large oak tree with Fala, and could not remember the last time he had felt so relaxed. Earlier that morning, Fala had explained more about Okawna's heritage, and the ceremony had given him a much deeper appreciation for the Native Americans and their philosophies.

He heard Halona laughing and looked over at her dancing around a sitting calico cat, which was ignoring her, and it felt as if they were a family. He was already dreading having to go home tomorrow, but at least he had one more night in their company.

Chapter 26

SATURDAY. COBRA:

When Chris heard a truck approaching through the woods, he climbed out of the golf cart, ready to meet his new passenger. He knew it was a woman, but was not told the reason for her visit. When the truck stopped, the driver climbed out, so he went over to introduce himself. When the passenger door opened, he was pleased to see she was attractive, and held out his hand. "I'm Chris Jenkins, your security guard."

Rita studied the hefty man before climbing out of the truck and accepting his hand. "Rita Harrow. Are you the only help I get?"

Chris hadn't realized he would be helping her. "As far as I know. I'll do what I can, but I'm just a security guard."

"All right, Chris. Give us a hand unloading this thing."

After the driver lowered the forklift to the ground, Chris opened the rear door of the truck and looked inside. His first impression was some type of experimental torpedo, and he wondered why they would bring it here. When he heard a beep from the forklift, he stepped out of the way as the driver slid the forks under the pallet holding the device. The lift raised it a few inches and then backed it out and set the torpedo onto a heavy-duty trailer behind the golf cart.

Chris helped Rita load several plastic cases into the back of the cart, and when the truck headed down the road through the woods, he drove them through the entrance and along a long tunnel. Once inside the main chamber, they used a powerful electric chain hoist to unload the torpedo, position it upright, and secure it to a fiberglass support frame. They unpacked her equipment and set it up on a console, and then she drove the golf cart out of the mountain and entered Preston's number.

"Hi, Steve. I'm ready to test the device. How soon can you get here?"

"Tomorrow afternoon, so just hold off until I arrive."

"All right. I guess I can wait."

"Good. I'll see you tomorrow."

When she entered the main chamber, Chris was dragging a power cord across the floor to the console. She studied the configurations for a moment and then looked at Chris. "I'm impressed. Are you really just a guard and not a technician?"

Chris grinned at the compliment. "I've hooked up enough computers and stereos to figure out what hooks up to what."

"Well, plug us in and let's see if this thing still works."

Chris felt a little uneasy, not knowing what was going on. "If you don't mind my asking. What is that thing? Is it a bomb? Can it blow up?"

Rita took a moment, trying to figure out what to tell him. "It's difficult to describe, but it's not explosive. Are you ready?"

"What should I expect?"

"We should see a small tornado form directly above the point. Here we go. Two, one, now."

Chris stared at the top of the torpedo, and was relieved when nothing happened. He didn't care what she said, the damn thing looked like a bomb, and bombs explode. "I guess it's a dud."

"I told you, it's not a bomb. I just have to try another set of frequencies tomorrow."

The lights flickered for a second, and Rita looked at Chris. "I thought this place ran on geothermal energy."

Chris looked around the room. "It's never done that before. It must have something to do with your non-bomb."

"That's ridiculous. It had nothing to do with it."

Chris shrugged his shoulders. "If you say so."

When Chris turned and strolled across the room toward the lounge, Rita stared after him as she considered his suggestion. She didn't completely understand how the devices functioned, or what might have caused the lights to flicker, but knew she had better figure out what went wrong before Steve arrived.

***

SUNDAY. COBRA:

When Chris drove down the tunnel with Preston, he had a bad feeling about the test today. He could sense Preston's excitement, although Rita seemed a little more reserved from her initial enthusiasm yesterday.

When the golf cart stopped near the steel door, Preston climbed out and strolled across the floor to Rita standing next to the control console. "Is everything ready?"

Rita smiled and reached out to pull him close for a hug and a kiss. It had been months since she had seen him, but he seemed so cold emotionally she thought he might have lost his affection for her.

When she let go, he was staring at the device. "Is something wrong?"

Preston thought of Rita as a puppet in his plan to make millions from cleanup contracts with the Federal and State Governments. "Of course not. I'm just eager to see if this thing works, is all."

Rita felt relieved his affection for her had not changed and smiled. "I'm all set."

When he heard the golf cart driving down the tunnel, Preston looked at Rita. "What's up with him?"

Rita understood why Chris had left, but didn't want to let Preston know she had ignored his order to wait. "Don't mind him. He's just a guard."

"All right. Show me how this thing works."

Rita turned it on, but nothing happened. "I don't understand. It should have worked."

The overhead lights suddenly exploded, sending shards of white hot metal raining down across the floor. When the alarm blared, the emergency lights flicked on, barely illuminating the vast room. The ground shook so hard the device toppled over, crashing onto the concrete. Rita and Preston grabbed the edge of the console for balance as the floor shuddered, then their hands were ripped from the console as the floor heaved up three inches, tossing them off their feet.

Rita held her arms up for protection as chunks of concrete crashed down from the ceiling. She struggled to breathe in the dust clogged air, much less see more than two feet ahead. When the shaking stopped, she suddenly remembered the blaring alarm was for the door closing. She stumbled over the debris, trying to reach the narrowing gap between the door and the frame. In her rush, she tripped over something soft on the floor and crashed onto the jagged pieces of concrete. "Shit!"

She got back onto her hands and knees and looked over at the door, just as a small sliver of light blinked out, and a deep thud filled the room. She remembered the keypad and stood to go try it, but realized what had caused her to fall. Preston's body was buried under pieces of shattered rock from the ceiling, and a puddle of blood had spread out from under his head.

She stared at the dark buttons on the control pad, but realized she didn't even know the combination. At first, she laughed, but when reality set in, she leaned back against the cold steel door and slowly slid down onto the floor.

She brought her knees up under her chin and wrapped her arms around her legs as tears welled up in her eyes. She could only hope Chris would let someone know what happened, but then she realized he would probably tell them a bomb had caused the earthquake, and she was dead. There would be no rush to open the door, and they would probably just leave it as a crypt. She wrapped her arms over her eyes and sobbed.

***

Chris had just cleared the exit when the Golf cart rocked from side to side, and realized it was an earthquake only a second before it rolled over, tossing him to the ground. When he looked up above the entrance, massive boulders of gray rock were rolling down the face of the mountain. He scrambled onto his feet and ran down the road, and when he glanced over his shoulder, saw thick gray dust roiling out from the entrance of the facility.

***

SUNDAY. OKAWNA RANCH:

His bag was already in his SUV, but Alex kept procrastinating to leave as he and Fala sat under the tree. His second night at the ranch had been even better that the first. "How about you and Halona come and stay at my place next weekend? I have a spare bedroom, and I'd love to show both of you around Bozeman."

Fala was hoping Alex would like to see her and Halona again, and he wasn't too far from where they lived in West Yellowstone. "We'd love to."

They both turned when they heard high-pitched giggling and watched Okawna swinging Halona in a circle by the arms. When Alex grinned and looked back at her, Fala leaned in close, kissing him lightly on the lips. When she leaned back, Alex felt everything was right in the universe and smiled at her. They stopped when they felt the ground tremble, and stood to look around as if they might see the cause, but everything seemed fine.

Judith stepped out of the kitchen onto the back porch and looked down at Alex. "What just happened?"

"It was an earthquake, but I don't understand why. This part of Wyoming is geologically stable. I'll make a quick call to a friend and find out if he knows anything about it."

Alex brought out his phone and selected a contact. "Hey, Jerry. Did you just have a seismic event in the park?"

"Not that I'm aware of, but I'm at home right now. Let me call the park headquarters and check. I'll call you back when I find out."

"Thanks."

Okawna looked at Alex. "What's going on?"

"I'm not sure."

As if on cue, Alex's phone rang. "I'm here, Jerry."

"We had a tremor, but everything seems to be okay. We get them all the time, remember?"

"All right. Thanks."

Alex grinned at everyone. "It came from Yellowstone, but there's nothing to worry about. I guess it was telling me to stop delaying the inevitable and start heading home."

Fala smiled as she wrapped her arms around Alex's neck, holding him close. "I'll be staying here with Judith and Okawna for a few more days before going home, but we'll see you next Saturday."

"I look forward to it."

When Alex stepped back, Halona was smiling up at him with her arms wide, so he grabbed her under the arms and cradled her on his forearm. "I'll see you next Saturday."

"You promise?"

"I promise."

When she wrapped her arms around his neck, he held her close, already missing her. When he set her down, he received a hug from Judith and Okawna.

"Thanks for your hospitality, Judith."

"You're always welcome. Drive safely."

It seemed the hardest thing he ever had to do as he climbed into his SUV. He stared at them, looking at him, as he started the engine, and then watched them in the rearview mirror as he drove away.

Chapter 27

MONDAY MORNING. USGS MAMMOTH STATION:
When Jerry arrived at the seismic center, Vivian and Paul gave him troubled expressions. "What's going on?"

Paul pointed at the monitor. "The GPS unit at the Thumb geyser basin shows a two-inch increase in elevation, and we're getting reports from the rangers of unusually violent geyser eruptions. Dozens of burn victims are waiting for transportation to the nearest hospitals."

"Oh, my God! Any idea why this happened?"

Vivian shook her head no. "It's a strange coincidence this happened right after the tremor yesterday. There has to be a connection."

They heard the soft beeping from another GPS unit and looked at the monitor, and the flashing red light was on the southeast edge of the park. Another flashing red light appeared on the southern edge, and then another on the northeast edge.

The desk phone rang as several touchpad lights flashed, and Vivian pressed the button for the speaker and connected with one of the incoming calls. "This is the USGS."

A panicky voice came from the speaker. "I can see an ash plume about thirty miles east of the park and it looks like a small eruption! What is going on?"

Vivian looked at Jerry. "What do you want me to say?"

Jerry stepped closer to the phone. "We don't know, but I suggest you leave the area immediately."

Jerry pressed another button. "USGS."

"Jerry, it's Myra. Old faithful is out of control! The victims are overwhelming us in the hotel and we're not prepared to handle this kind of situation. What's going on?"

"We don't know, Myra. It's happening all over the park. Tell anyone who can drive to take as many people as possible out of the area. I'm closing the park."

Jerry received a nod from Paul, who grabbed his cell phone to call the park Director. Jerry looked at Vivian. "You handle the incoming calls while I call Alex Cave."

***

BOZEMAN COLLEGE:

When his cellphone vibrated in his pocket, Alex was in the middle of a discussion with his freshman students and tried to ignore it, but it stopped and started again, so he apologized and turned away from the students to answer. "What's going on, Jerry?"

"We're getting reports from all over the park. The caldera is becoming active and we can't figure out why. I need your help."

"What can I do?"

"It's too difficult to explain over the phone. Get here as fast as you can, so you can see for yourself."

"I'm on my way."

Alex ended the call and looked at his students, wondering what to tell them without causing a panic. "I have an emergency and need to leave. I'll see you tomorrow."

As his students left the classroom, Alex locked his desk, grabbed his briefcase, and headed for the parking lot. He thought about the tremor he felt at the ranch yesterday as he climbed in and started the engine, and then he headed for Yellowstone.

Chapter 28

GROOM LAKE, NEVADA:

David was strolling across the warehouse floor and noticed the surface of the sphere was shimmering, as if a liquid, but abruptly stopped when a bald man stepped out. "Whoa!"

"Hello, David. I'm Paladin, and we've already met. Tell me what's going on right now."

David stared with his mouth hanging open for a moment. "You're one of the missing crew from the spaceship."

"No, I'm not. Now tell me what's happening on this planet right now."

David wasn't sure what to say. "Where did you come from?"

"It's a long story. Where is Alex?"

"Um, I'm not sure. At the college, I guess. How do you know Alex?"

Paladin sighed with relief. "It must have worked this time. Can you call him to be sure?"

"Yeah, but what do you mean, it worked this time?"

"I'll explain later, now make the call."

David brought out his phone and selected a contact. "What do you want me to say?"

"Ask him if he's okay."

It took several rings before Alex answered. "I'm in a hurry, David, so make it fast."

"Is everything okay?"

"No, it's not. How did you know?"

"I didn't. I was asked to call and find out if you were okay. What's going on?"

"Yellowstone is becoming active, so I'm headed to the park to help find out why."

David looked at Paladin. "He says Yellowstone is active."

"Tell him he needs to get here right away."

David stared at him for a moment. "I don't understand. He's heading to the park to help. That's where he's needed right now."

"Tell him you are sending a helicopter to pick him up before it's too late."

David stared back with a bewildered expression. He felt conflicted, unsure of what to do first.

Paladin grew impatient. "There is no time to explain, so just tell him, David!"

"Alex? A helicopter is coming to pick you up and bring you down here to the base."

"Who's sending a helicopter, and why do I need to go down there?"

"It's a man who came out of the silver sphere. His name is Mister Paladin, and he says he knows you."

"I don't have time for twenty questions, David. I don't know anyone named Paladin. Did you say from the sphere?"

"Yeah, he walked out of it."

Paladin held his hand out for the phone and David gave it to him. "There is no time to explain, Alex. You need to trust me on this."

"Who is this?"

"I'm Paladin. I'm a time traveler, and I've seen your future. An eruption is imminent, and you're the only one who can change the outcome. You need to trust me about this. When the helicopter arrives, you must leave immediately and get back here."

Alex was just pulling up to the seismic activity center at Mammoth Station. "I don't care who you are. I can't just leave."

"If you want to save your friend Okawna and the woman, you had better do as I ask."

Alex had just opened the car door, but didn't get out. "How do you know about my friends? Did David tell you?"

"Like I said. I'm a time traveler. I know all about you and your friends, so do what I ask, or everyone you care about will die during the eruption."

Alex sat in numbed silence for a moment, wondering if this person was legitimate, and how could he possibly know about his friends. "Tell David I'm at the Mammoth station in the park. He'll know where it is. Send the helicopter and I'll be waiting."

Paladin gave the phone back to David. "Call whoever you need to and send a helicopter to someplace called Mammoth Station in the park."

The only person David could think of to call was Alex's friend, Martin Donner. He entered the number, wondering how he was going to explain this to the Director of National Security without sounding like a crackpot.

***

USGS MAMMOTH STATION:

Jerry turned from the wall monitor when he heard the door open and Alex walk in. "I appreciate your help."

Alex nodded hello to Vivian and Paul and then turned to Jerry and the monitor. "Where's the latest activity?"

"We've just had another eruption north of the park, so that makes five. It all started with the tremor yesterday, but it wasn't powerful enough to start something of this magnitude. None of it makes sense."

"We knew it was overdue, but you're right. We would have noticed a steady increase in activity long before now."

"I've already started evacuating the park, but these new eruptions are creating the zipper effect, so I don't think we have much time left before it blows."

Alex suddenly thought about the Okawna ranch and moved to another map. According to the latest estimates, the blast zone will be five hundred miles, and he discovered the ranch was fifty miles too close.

He turned back to Jerry. "If this thing blows, you're going with it unless you leave right now. There's nothing you can do to stop it."

Jerry turned to look at Vivian and Paul, who nodded their heads in agreement. "Both of you leave right now."

When they ran from the room, Jerry turned back to Alex. "It's going to take some time getting five-hundred-miles from here."

"I'm not sure if it will happen in time, but supposedly, I have a helicopter on the way, so you're going with me."

When Alex tried to call the ranch to warm them, all he heard was static. "Do your hardline telephones work?"

"Not anymore. Too much static electricity in the air from the eruptions."

When the building swayed for an instant, Alex motioned toward the door. "It's getting ready to blow. No sense waiting in here to get crushed."

Alex stepped out from the building and the hairs on his arms stood up, and then the ground shifted beneath his feet. A deep rumble seemed to hang in the air, drowning out the sound of helicopter blades until it was nearly on top of him. He looked up and waved it down to the parking lot while he grabbed his bag from his SUV. When it landed, it only took a moment for him and Jerry to climb inside, and then the military pilot took off and quickly gained altitude.

Alex slid a set of headphones over his ears so he could talk to the pilots. "What are your orders?"

The copilot turned in her seat. "We're to fly you down to Nevada."

"We need to make a stop first. Head southeast to Stillwater, Wyoming."

"I've flown over that area, so no problem."

"I really appreciate it."

Alex noticed Jerry's slumped body position and the sadness in his eyes. "There was nothing you could have done to stop this, my friend."

The copilot turned in her seat. "We're coming up on Stillwater, Mister Cave."

"Start heading due east. We're looking for a small ranch on road sixty-three."

When the pilot did as requested, Alex leaned forward to look through the front window. In the distance, he could barely see the house and relaxed, knowing he was going to make it in time.

The proximity alarm blared from the speaker just as Jerry gasped. "Look!"

When they looked north through the side window, a roiling cloud of desert sand was rushing in their direction. The Pilot instinctively gained altitude and swung the helicopter away from the blast wave, and when Alex lost sight of the ranch, he knew it was about to be demolished.

Every muscle in his body strained against the other as he fought hard to keep his anguish in check. A moment later, he felt the helicopter become level again and stared out the window, desperately hoping something of the ranch remained to save his friend's lives.

Once the shock wave had passed, a thick layer of dust settled a few feet above the ground, but there was nothing left standing for miles in all directions. When he suddenly saw a stone chimney, Alex sat up and turned to the co-pilot. "I see something. Turn east."

She turned in her seat. "Nothing could have survived, Mister Cave."

"My family lives there and I have to be sure. Please."

When the pilot changed direction, Alex stared through the front window, trying to locate the chimney again. "Over there, just to the north. See the chimney?"

A few moments later, the blades swept away the dirt cloud over the house, and Alex tried hard to suppress his sense of hope. A corner area of the basement where the floor had collapsed could have been enough to shield anyone from the direct blast.

He turned to the pilot. "Set us down."

Before the helicopter touched the ground, Alex leapt out the side door, running toward the basement. "It's Alex! Can anyone hear me?"

When no one answered, he ripped away the loose debris leaning against the corner. "Is anyone alive?"

He strained to lift a large section of the collapsed floor, but it wouldn't budge. Suddenly Jerry was at his side, and they flipped it out of the way.

When Alex turned back to see what was left, his knees seemed to lose their strength as he slowly slumped to the ground. Pieces of splintered wood were covered in blood, most of them sticking out of the four bodies on the ground.

Alex hardly noticed Jerry rush past him until he was checking for any signs of life, and then watched in numbed silence. When Jerry stood to face him, the look in his eyes told him what he needed to know.

Jerry placed his hand on his friend's shoulder. "I'm very sorry, Alex."

Alex regained his composure and stood up, but he couldn't hide his rage. He reached down and grabbed a loose board, and then roared in anger as he hurled it into the air. As it flew from his hand, one nail ripped through his shirt, gouging his skin along the message on his forearm.

As the pain throbbed, the dark cloud in the back of his mind disappeared, and he was overwhelmed by the flood of images racing through his memory. A moment later, everything seemed apparent as he remembered Paladin, then he looked at Jerry. "Why didn't it work?"

Jerry just stared at Alex. "What didn't work?"

Alex's hands clenched into fists. "Never mind. It's time to go,"

Alex stomped across to the helicopter and he and Jerry climbed in. Once they were airborne, the pilot headed for Salt Lake City to drop off his friend before catching a flight to Nevada.

The thumping of the rotor blades became hypnotic, and Alex felt emotionally drained as he slumped in his chair. A small tear slowly slipped down his cheek as the same question played over and over in his thoughts. He had taken the radio from Rita as planned, so why didn't it work?

Before he realized it, the copilot informed them they were landing at the airport. The helicopter set down away from the other aircraft, and Alex thanked them for their help. As he and Jerry climbed out, a government vehicle pulled up, so they got into the back seat.

It was a short drive to the air terminal, where the driver waited while they got out. Alex gave Jerry a hug, knowing there wasn't much to say, and then stepped back.

Jerry stared up at his friend. "Thanks for the rescue. Good luck."

"You, too, Jerry."

Once Jerry entered the terminal, Alex got back into the vehicle. "Where are we headed?"

"To a secure hangar, where a special plane is waiting to fly you to Groom Lake."

"That's the best news I've had all day."

Chapter 29

GROOM LAKE, NEVADA:
The special plane stopped in front of the security terminal, and since Alex was the only passenger, he had made friends with the pilot and copilot during the flight. He said goodbye before grabbing his bag and going down the stairs, and continued into the building and through the checkpoint.

David watched Alex pass through security without issue, but when he stopped in front of him, the look on Alex's face broke his heart. "I'm really sorry about Okawna. I really liked him."

"I know. Thanks. Where's Paladin?"

"He's waiting in Henry's office."

"I need to make a stop on the way."

"No problem. I have a golf cart waiting outside."

"Good. Let's go."

***

Alex led David into Henry's office. "Hello, Paladin."

Paladin grinned. "You remember this time? Good."

Alex rolled up his bloodied sleeve. "I stopped Rita just like we planned, so why didn't it work?"

"As long as everything revolves around finding and touching the sphere, too many variables come into play, each with a different result."

"Then how come you can do it with such precision?"

"My suit. It allows me to enter the machine and decide where I need to be."

When Alex opened a plastic bag and tossed the silver suit onto the desk, Paladin stood and snatched it up while staring at Alex. "Where did you get this?"

"I found it in the cargo hold of a spaceship. It was occupied."

"You found the first traveler? Is she okay?"

"I'm afraid not. The body had turned to dust and fell through the material when I picked up the suit."

"It reacts to living tissue. She was the first traveler, and we sent her back to find out what happened to this planet. She was supposed to retrieve the advanced technology the first race of humans to live here had left behind. We never learned what happened to her." He tossed the suit onto the desk. "See if it fits."

"I know it will. What have you got in mind?"

"Wearing the suit will allow you to enter the sphere. Once you're inside, I can set the machine to send you to a specific place and time, and you will still remember the mission."

David reached out and took the suit. "That's nice material. You said she was the first time traveler. What happened?"

"She never returned to our time period, so we never found out, until now. We still don't know what went wrong."

Alex took the suit back. "If I'm going to get it right this time, I need a plan for when I come out. Preferably someplace where I can change into normal clothes."

Henry had an idea. "Everything was set in motion once the Mystic activated the first device, so we need to make the change before then."

Paladin knew Henry was correct. "Destinations in time travel can be determined by a specific event, so you must change the order of events just prior to the activation, or a similar timeline will be set in motion."

"Send me back a few days earlier and I'll stop the Mystic before they activate the device."

Paladin shook his head no. "There are too many variables between the time you arrive and when you can stop the event. It has to be a matter of minutes, not days, nor even hours."

"Just make sure I come out near a phone."

"You will need more than a phone."

Alex noticed Paladin's sly grin. "Is something funny?"

"No. Amusing, perhaps. When you arrive, you will be naked."

"Won't I be wearing the suit?"

"The suit allows you to pass through the sphere, and once inside, your memories will be accessed by the computer for a specific location from your recent past. I can't allow you to keep the suit, Alex, so you must remove it prior to my sending you back. I'll try to make it somewhere secluded."

"Can't I wear it over my clothes?"

"No. The suit reacts to living tissue and must be against your skin to work."

"Fine. Send me home and I'll call Okawna."

"We've been through this before, Alex. Do you know the precise time of the activation?"

"Okawna told me when I was on the Mystic. My memories are cluttered in my head right now, and everything happened differently each time, so it's difficult separating each event. Just give me a minute to remember." Alex stared off into space for a moment and then grinned. "Monday, two weeks ago. 9:00 AM."

"Exactly 9:00 AM?"

"It's the best I can do."

"I can get you within five minutes of either side, but that's the best I can do. This is the last attempt, Alex. According to our time travel laws, I'm not allowed to interfere, but I have violated the law three times for you already, and when I return, I will be forced to face the consequences of my actions. Our governing council is not very forgiving in these matters."

"Like I said. Just get me close to a phone. Oh, make sure it's not a pay phone. I won't have any change when I arrive."

"Where were you on Monday at eight fifty-five AM? Perhaps your college? It should amuse your students when you instantly become naked right in front of their eyes."

"True, but my first class starts at 1:00 PM, so I don't leave the house until noon on Mondays."

"Very well. Your home it is. Are you ready?"

Alex grabbed the suit as he stood. "I'd better not change before we get to the hangar. You can get away with walking around in a pretty suit because nobody knows who you are. According to a young nurse, some misguided people around here think I'm some kind of legend."

David stood and grinned. "I wonder why?"

"That will change if I can stop the Mystic. Okay. Let's do this."

***

When they entered the warehouse, Alex stared at the sphere. "Did anyone figure out why the spaceship carrying this thing crashed?"

"No, the first traveler didn't return, remember? I was sent to find her and recover the devices. When I learned what was happening on this planet, I decided to break our law and help you."

When Alex turned and headed for a private office to change, Henry turned to Paladin and realized they were nearly the same height. "Forgive my curiosity, but are you of normal stature among your people? The spaceship seemed much larger than necessary for your physical size."

"Yes, this is normal. Over eons of evolution, our need for physical size to survive became unnecessary. Now fewer resources are required to accommodate our needs."

"That makes sense."

David turned when the door to the office opened. When Alex stepped out wearing the suit, he clapped his hands. "Now you look like a real superhero."

Alex grinned. "You're a funny man, David. Let's get this over with?"

When everyone stopped next to the sphere, Alex looked at his friends. "I guess it's not really goodbye. I'll see you later."

David held out his hand, and Alex shook it. "Good luck."

Alex gave Henry a hug. "When I get back, we'll go to spaceship and fly it here. See you soon."

Paladin hesitated to step into the sphere. "I must warn you, Alex. Knowledge of future events can be dangerous to you, and those who will take advantage of what you know. You must tell no one how you acquired your information."

"No one will do what I ask if I can't tell them why."

"You must rely on the people who will trust you without reservation."

"All right. I know of two who will help me. Let's go."

Paladin stared at Alex. "Even if this works, it will be a new timeline, so be very careful about changing things that should not be changed. The events you set in motion could cause a worse scenario than what should have happened. You may believe everything will return to normal, but in my limited experience with time travel, it never turns out the way I planned."

"I'll take my chances."

"Stop thinking about yourself! You must think about how your actions will affect the rest of humanity! Do not take this responsibility lightly!"

Alex knew Paladin was right. "Okay. Let's do this."

Henry suddenly had a question. "One moment, Paladin. What about those devices? What is the secret for making them work?"

"They do not work as intended, Henry. I suspect they were the reason the spaceship crashed, but I cannot be sure. Bring them here and once they are all in one place, I will receive a signal and come back to get them."

When Paladin stepped into the sphere, Alex gave his friends a brief wave and followed him through the surface. An instant later, the warehouse was empty.

Chapter 30

BOZEMAN, MONTANA:

Alex suddenly realized he was in the meadow down near the pond behind his barn, and it felt like his left forearm was on fire. "Damn!"

In an instant, the pain was gone, so he brought his arm up, knowing exactly why. The pain was from the new scar of the nail that had ripped his shirt open, and the pink skin formed a ragged sword slicing through a lightning storm. To anyone else, there was no message.

He felt a cool breeze flow across his butt and realized he was naked. As he ran up the hill toward the house, his dog barked once to let him know he was watching.

"Hey, boy. It's just me."

When he reached the porch, he gave Barney a quick pat hello and ran into the living room. The wall clock showed 8:59 as he grabbed his phone off the counter and entered Okawna's number. Four rings went by without an answer as the clock chimed 9:00 AM.

After eight rings, he got Okawna's voice mail. "Okawna, it's Alex. I know you're on the Mystic, but do not use the ultrasound. I repeat, do not use the ultrasound, and call me immediately when you get this message. It's extremely important, so don't let me down. I'll explain later."

He looked up, and the clock showed 9:01. "Come on, Okawna. Call me."

When he glanced in the mirror, Alex realized he was still naked and hurried down the hall to his bedroom. When he returned to the living room, the clock showed 9:08. "Come on, come on. Call me."

He slipped the phone into his shirt pocket and went out onto the back porch with Barney. He searched for every idea he could think of, but there was no other way to stop the Mystic.

His wristwatch showed 9:15, and he was losing hope he would succeed. He slumped down onto a porch chair and Barney licked his fingers, but it was of little comfort. He checked and his watch now showed 9:20.

When he heard the first ring, he leapt out of the chair and answered. "Did you get my message?"

"Yeah, a few minutes ago. What's going on?"

"The ultra sound? Is it off?"

"It's off, all right? Now, tell me what's going on. How did you know I was on the Mystic?"

Alex let his shoulders relax. "It's a long story, my friend. One better told in private. For now, do not activate the ultra sound no matter what anyone says."

"Sure. I could ask Mike to head back into port if you like?"

"Really? You can get him to do that for you?"

"Yes, but when I get off this phone, I had better have a damn good reason for stopping his new project."

"It's a matter of national security, and I mean that in a big way. You have no idea how big, and don't trust Dieter, Bartram, or Rita. Keep an eye on Harrison, too."

"That's most of the crew, but I'll deal with it. I don't know if national security will fly as a reason for Mike to stop the experiment, either."

"Tell him to expect a call from our friend, Donner. I'm going to make a secure video call to him in a few minutes, and then I plan to fly out to join you and give you the details when I arrive."

"You're scaring me, Alex. How do you know everyone on the Mystic?"

"I'll explain everything when I get there, so have a cold beer waiting for me. I'll see you this afternoon."

Alex walked back into the house and entered his office and then turned on the computer, and it took several minutes to establish a secure connection to the Director's office. A moment later, Donner's image appeared on the screen. "You have no idea how glad I am to see you, Martin."

"This is a surprise. You look a little worried."

"I know, but I need a favor and you're going to have to trust me on what I'm about to tell you. During the debriefing of the Dead Energy operation, I told you about a spaceship that had crashed with some strange devices. Do you remember?"

"How could I forget? The circumstances were bizarre, to say the least. They were going to use them to clean the atmosphere, correct?"

"That's right. I've found the spacecraft, Martin. I also know the location of three of the alien devices."

"How? Where are they?"

"The 'how' is the problem. No disrespect, but I cannot tell you. I can only ask that you trust me on this."

"What are you asking me to do, Alex?"

"Okawna is working for a man named Mike Tanner, a wealthy researcher with good intentions. I want to use his research equipment to retrieve two of the devices. One is off the coast of Washington State, and I know the exact location. The other is in the Arctic Ocean. I don't know where exactly, but with the help of the crew on Mike's research ship, the Mystic, we can pinpoint the location and use his equipment to retrieve the device."

"What do you need from me?"

"For the moment, only a phone call. Call Mike and ask for his assistance, but only tell him it's top secret and a matter of national security. Explain who I am, and that everything will be coordinated through Okawna and me."

"Won't he want to be paid for his services?"

"He's a rare breed, Martin. He has plenty of money and uses it for the benefit of humanity. Hard to believe, I know, but it's true. Okawna has the security clearance, so he'll be in charge of the operation and be dealing directly with me, so your involvement with that part of the operation will be minimal."

"What's the other part?"

"I need complete secrecy to recover a spaceship. It's in an isolated location and we'll fly it to Nevada at night."

"How do you know all this, Alex?"

"I can't tell you. I'm sorry, but you'll just have to trust me."

"If I ask for military support, I need a good reason."

"No military involvement, Martin. Too many people will need to know what I'm doing. All I need is Doctor Henry Heinz at Area 51, and a helicopter. And your approval, of course. Oh, and temporary use of your jet while I get everything organized."

"If it was anyone but you, Alex, I'd demand an explanation. You did a great job on the Dead Energy project, so I'll leave it in your capable hands. Oh, I almost forgot. I'll send you the background checks you asked for. It's an interesting read."

"Thanks."

Alex ended the call and looked down at his dog on the floor beside him. "Sorry, Barney, but I can't stick around. I'll call Judy and ask her to stop by while I'm gone."

Chapter 31

DARRINGTON, WASHINGTON:

Sasha held an envelope out to Boris. "Here is a photograph of the boy, Derek, but I cannot find one for the girl."

"They are brother and sister, so if the boy is eighteen, she will be sixteen or seventeen. They'll be at the high school, so take Mikhail and bring them here. I'll pay a visit to Cave's father."

"Rudolf is watching the house in Montana and will let us know if Cave leaves."

"Good. After Rudolf calls, tell him to stay there. I don't want him screwing things up out here."

***

BOZEMAN MONTANA:

Rudolf had been watching Cave's house since early this morning, but what he thought happened half an hour ago was not possible. He knew for sure Cave was in the house, and yet he was suddenly running up from the field, naked. He thought about calling Sasha and telling her what happened, but knew she would not believe him, and Boris was already looking for an excuse to get rid of him. No, he decided. It would be his secret.

***

Alex still wasn't sure if it was over and entered Wesley Patterson's number. He was asked to leave a message and almost said Wesley. "Mister Patterson. My name is Alex

Cave. We met at a conference in Iceland a few months ago. Could you please call me?"

It only took a few seconds before his phone rang. "Thanks for calling back, Mister Patterson."

"I remember you, Alex. We sat with that attractive blond woman, Sonja."

"That's right. Did you notice any seismic activity over the past hour?"

"Nothing here. Why do you ask?"

"I used to live in that area, and I was curious."

"I know your father, Robert. As far as I know, everything's quiet around here."

"Okay. Thanks. I'll stop and see you when I get the chance."

***

Rudolf followed Cave to the airport. When a private jet picked him up, he could no longer follow him and called Sasha.

Chapter 32

SEATTLE, WASHINGTON:
During the flight, Alex thought about how to repair his relationship with his father. In this new timeline, there was no longer a desperate situation to bring them together. His only option would be to talk to Derek and Kristy about what had happened to their parents, and perhaps they would help mend the pain in his father's heart so they could be a family again.

***

SPARROW VALLEY HIGH SCHOOL:
Sasha was staring through the tinted window of the van at the boy's motorcycle in the parking lot, and then looked over at Mikhail in the passenger seat. "Boris should be with Cave's father by now. I'm sure he's telling him we already have the children, so we had better not fail or he will kill you."

***

CAVE RANCH:
When Robert Cave heard a vehicle coming up the road, he looked out through the screened door as a dark blue sedan stopped in the driveway. He stood from the kitchen table and went out onto the porch as the car door opened, and a tall, slender man climbed out. From his profile, he would be considered handsome. When he turned, Robert saw an oval-shaped ring of scar tissue encircling a large area of his left cheek. "What can I do for you?"

Boris took his time looking around before staring at Robert. "I have your grandchildren, and I came here to repay a debt owed to me by your son, Alex."

Robert felt numbed by his answer. "Who are you?"

"I'm Boris Kinski, and your son killed my brother."

Robert's hands clenched into fists at his sides. "Did you kill my other son, Ken?"

"Of course. A brother for a brother, but it's just not enough. He ruined my life, and I will only be satisfied when he sees his family tortured before his eyes."

"Then take me. I raised him, so this is between you and me. Leave my grandkids out of this."

"The way I hear it, you hate Alex anyway, so torturing you won't have the same effect."

When Robert didn't reply, Boris held a note out to him. "Tell him to call me at this number. I will give him four hours, or I'll kill the girl to prove I'm serious."

"Four hours? That might be hard to do. I don't know where he is."

"I've just received a call from one of my men. Your son should arrive in Seattle soon."

Robert glared at Kinski as he took the note. "Nice scar. Did my boy give that to you?"

When he saw the anger in Boris's eyes, Robert grinned and Boris slapped him, but he was still grinning when he turned back to face him. "Is that the best you can do?"

Boris's eyes hardened into piercing orbs as he reached into his pocket and pulled out a pistol, aiming it at Robert. "I doubt seeing the remains of your grandchildren will be so humorous. He has four hours."

When Boris slid the pistol into his pocket and drove away from the ranch, Robert ran into the house to get his wallet and keys. When he came out, he was also holding a rifle as he ran across to the garage to get his pickup.

***

SPARROW VALLEY HIGH SCHOOL:

When Jessica Parker stopped him in the hallway, Derek Cave leaned back against the lockers. "Why won't you leave me alone, Jessica?"

She lightly shook her hair and smiled. "You just seem so lonely all the time."

Derek knew it was time to tell her how he felt and leaned away from the lockers. "Don't you get it? You and I are related."

Jessica's smile slipped away. "What do you mean?"

"My mother was your aunt. That makes us cousins, so we can't have that kind of relationship."

Derek turned and stomped down the hallway. When he reached the doors, he slammed his palms against the handle, threw the door open, and stomped across the grass. He liked her too, but as a friend and she had to stop chasing him for that kind of relationship.

***

When Sasha recognized Derek's face from the picture, she rolled the window partway down and peered through the gap to make sure. "It is him! Get in back!"

***

Derek had just reached his motorcycle when he heard Jessica call his name and turned to look at her. When she stopped running, he crossed his arms and stared at her. "What do you want from me?"

"Well, I was thinking you still need a friend."

Derek uncrossed his arms. "That's more like it. Would you like to go for a ride on my motorcycle?"

Jessica smiled. "I was hoping you'd ask me. Sure."

Her smile slipped away when a dark blue van suddenly stopped behind Derek. When Derek saw the curious look in Jessica's eyes, he turned around to see why. The side door of a cargo van suddenly opened and a tough-looking man waved a gun at him. He felt Jessica's arm wrap around his as the side window went down, then a dark-haired woman pointed a gun with a silencer in his direction.

Sasha waved the end of the pistol toward the open side door. "Get in the van!"

Derek slid his arm out of Jessica's and took a step toward the woman. "I think you have the wrong person."

"I know exactly who you are, Derek Cave. Both of you get in before I shoot one of you to prove I'm serious."

Jessica grabbed his arm, pulling him back as she glared at the woman. "My uncle's the sheriff, so leave us alone!"

Derek spun around to face Jessica. "What are you doing? Run!"

Mikhail leapt out of the van and pointed the gun at Derek's face. "Both of you get in!"

Sasha waited until the kids climbed in and the door was closed, and then stepped on the accelerator, racing out of the parking lot.

After fastening zip-ties around their hands and feet, Mikhail climbed into the passenger seat and looked at Sasha. "Do you want me to gag them?"

"No. Did you hear what she said? She's not his sister, and the police will be looking for her."

"It was taking too long. What would you have me do, shoot her in the parking lot? Drive us into the woods and I will get rid of her."

Jessica leaned against Derek's shoulder. "Don't let them kill me!"

Derek recognized the accent and thought about his uncle. Robert had insisted the Russians had killed his parents because of something Alex had done, but it was never proven. He leaned close to Jessica's ear. "It's my fault you're involved in this, and I'm sorry."

"They sound like foreigners, so how could you be involved?"

"It's not me. It's my uncle Alex. They're after me because of something he did. That's why my parents were murdered."

Jessica noticed Derek wiggling his hands together. "What are you doing?"

"I want to move the long piece of this strap around so I can pull it tight with my teeth."

"Why? You won't be able to break it."

"Just keep quiet, all right?"

Jessica tried to convince herself this was not real, only a dream. When she felt Derek struggling with the wrist straps, she knew it was real and leaned back against the van as tears blurred her vision.

***

SPARROW VALLEY GRADE SCHOOL:

When Robert drove into the parking lot, he saw Kristy's yellow backpack on the ground. He slammed the gears into park and leapt out of the truck, desperately searching the school grounds for his little sweetheart.

"Grandpa?"

Robert spun around, his heart nearly bursting when Kristy walked up to him, so he knelt down and wrapped her in his arms. "Thank goodness you're safe."

"What are you doing here?"

Robert let go and looked into her eyes. "Have you seen Derek recently?"

"No, but he's probably hiding from Jessica Parker."

Robert grabbed her backpack and stood. "Get in the truck, sweetie. We're going to find him."

***

SPARROW VALLEY HIGH SCHOOL:

When Robert and Kristie arrived, Derek's motorcycle was still in the parking lot, and Kristy pointed through the window. "That's Jessica's mustang over there. Maybe they're still inside."

"Stay close to me and we'll look around."

Robert opened his door and climbed out and then helped Kristi down onto the gravel, then they continued across the parking lot and entered the building. The hallway was deserted, so they looked into every room and discovered three students working on a project in the biology lab. "I'm looking for my grandson, Derek. Have any of you seen him?"

A girl raised her hand. "I saw him a little while ago, Mister Cave. He and Jessica Parker were headed to the parking lot."

"If they show up, have him call me right away."

As they walked out of the room, Kristy grabbed Robert's hand. "Is Derek in trouble, Grandpa?"

"I'm afraid so. I'd better go find the sheriff."

Chapter 33

ANACORTES MARINA:

Alex drove his rental sedan into the parking lot and recognized the Mystic anchored in a large open area of water, about sixty yards offshore. He stopped in front of marina office and climbed out as Okawna and Mike strolled over to greet him.

Okawna gave Alex a hug. "Would you mind telling me what's going on?"

Alex looked at Mike and reached out to shake hands. "I appreciate this."

Mike accepted. "Nice to meet you, Alex. Would you mind telling me why I had to stop my tests?"

"In a moment. Is the rest of the crew still onboard?"

"No, I asked Bett to take Lisa shopping. I was worried if there was trouble, she might get hurt."

Alex felt a small sense of relief. "Good idea. Let's go out to the Mystic and I'll tell you what's going on."

The trio headed for the end of the dock and climbed into the motorboat, and then Okawna drove them out to the Mystic. Alex tied the bow rope to a cleat and climbed out onto the stern deck. When he looked up at the bridge, Dieter was standing at the rear railing, watching them, and he turned to Mike. "Why don't both of you join me in your private quarters?"

Okawna and Mike exchanged puzzled stares, and Okawna shrugged. "I didn't tell him, Mike."

Alex knew what they were about to ask, so held up his hand. "I'll tell you once we have some privacy."

Mike indicated the door in to the ship. "This way."

Alex froze in mid-stride when Rita walked out on deck. Even though everything had changed, he couldn't forget about what happened in the other timelines, and it took every ounce of his self-restraint not to knock her on her butt.

Rita was ready to smile at the handsome stranger, but the second she was close enough to look into his eyes, a chill ran down her spine. She quickly turned away and walked up the stairs to the bridge.

Okawna had seen that look in Alex's eyes right before he killed the person he was looking at. "Alex? Are you okay?"

Alex realized he was still staring after Rita and turned toward the door. "I'm fine. Let's get inside."

Once seated in Mike's office, Alex tried to think of a way to explain what needed to be done without telling them why, and found it far more difficult than he had thought it would be. "I've recently discovered some information about two experimental devices lost at sea a very long time ago. This is classified information, so I can't go into any details about the experiment, but I would like your help, Mister Tanner. You have the equipment necessary to retrieve the devices, and since you don't have any political ties, you're the only person I can trust to handle this operation discreetly."

Tanner leaned back in his chair. "Call me Mike, and how do you know so much about me? I know we've never met."

"I'm sorry, but I'm not at liberty to say. Will you help me?"

Mike stared across the desk at Okawna, who indicated he thought it was okay, and then looked at Alex. "I like a good adventure. I'm in."

"Thanks."

"So, how do we get started?"

"First, we need to get rid of Dieter and his men. Bartram is wanted for several murders in the Netherlands, and Dieter gave the orders. Harrison is just a hired hand, but he's trouble waiting to happen."

"What should I tell them?"

Alex glanced over at his friend for a moment. "Nothing. Okawna and I will take them back to shore when we leave. I have warrants for Dieter and Bartram, and I'll give Harrison a subtle hint he should leave with us."

Okawna smirked. "I've seen your way of being subtle, Alex. You're almost as bad as me."

Alex grinned, then turned back to Mike and became serious. "You should get rid of Rita, too."

"That's most of my crew. Why Rita?"

"Have you ever heard of the DAR Corporation?"

Mike leaned back and crossed his arms. "They're a bunch of cutthroat bastards making millions off of other people's suffering."

"Rita's a spy for Steve Preston, the owner. Whatever you discover, she'll steal the plans for Preston. She has to go."

"All right."

Alex looked at Okawna. "When was the last time your father had a physical?"

Okawna's eyebrow went up. "I have no idea, why?"

"Call him right now and have him get a checkup at a hospital. Better yet. Call your mom and tell her to take him. Judith will make sure he goes in right away."

Okawna was stunned for a moment. "This is getting a little spooky, Alex. How do you know my mother? How do you know my dad needs to go to a hospital?"

Alex had already decided to change history by saving Okawna's father, despite Paladin's warning. He just hadn't thought about how to get it done without arousing suspicion and felt a little like a cornered rat. "I can't tell you. I'm sorry, but you'll just have to believe me and make the call."

Alex waited while Okawna left the room to make his call and then explained where the first device is located. "Use the methane as an excuse to be in the area with the Discovery."

***

Rita stared out the window at Okawna on the stern deck. So far, her plan to seduce him was working, and now was her opportunity to use his attraction to get information about the stranger.

Okawna finished calling his mom and saw Dieter and Rita staring down at him from the bridge. He didn't doubt Alex's word about who they were and what they were doing, but he wanted to find out for himself. He climbed the stairs, and when he stepped onto the bridge, Dieter and Rita stopped talking. He noticed Rita's seductive pose and knew what she was trying to do. He was being played, and did not like it.

Rita ran her hand through her hair and smiled. "What's going on, Okawna?"

"Just visiting with an old friend."

Dieter wondered the same thing. "What's his profession?"

"Why?"

Rita was glad Dieter was asking the questions. If Okawna had any suspicions, they would be directed at him, not her.

Dieter crossed his arms. "He has a certain look. Is he ex-military?"

Okawna grinned. "He's just a geology professor. Nothing for you to worry about."

"What's his name?"

Okawna was not about to give them any information. "Why are you so curious? Do you have something to hide?" When Dieter didn't answer, he knew what Alex had told him was true. "I thought so." He saw Rita look at the sat phone, so he grabbed it off the console, then frowned at her before going down the stairs.

Rita didn't know Dieter well enough to trust him, but knew something was going on. She decided to cover her own butt and let Dieter fend for himself, and used Okawna's leaving as an opportunity to leave the bridge.

Dieter knew this friend of Okawna's was more than just a teacher. He knew a professional killer when he saw one and left the bridge to find Bartram and Harrison. Until he knew more about what was going on, he was going to be ready for any new development.

***

When Okawna walked into Mike's office, Alex noticed the concern in his eyes. "Is everything all right?"

Okawna told Alex and Mike what happened on the bridge and then held up the phone. "I decided to keep this for a while."

When he saw the phone, Alex leaned back in his chair and released a slow breath of relief, since it was the crux of all the problems in the other time lines. "Dieter and his men have weapons, so we need to be careful when I arrest him and Bartram."

Mike slid open his top desk drawer. "I have a .45 caliber revolver."

Okawna smirked. "I have my .9 millimeter in my cabin."

Alex shook his head no. "I'd prefer not to get into a gunfight. We'll try to keep them separated." He felt his phone vibrate, slid it from his pocket, and recognized the caller ID. He was surprised and answered. "You never call me. What's wrong, Dad?"

"Damn you, Alex! This is your fault, just like getting your brother killed!"

"Just calm down and tell me what happened."

"They took Derek and the Parker girl. They were going to take Kristy, too, but I got to her first."

"Who took them?"

"A Russian named Boris Kinski. He said he's going to kill them unless you take their place."

Alex leaned back in his chair and rubbed his eyes for a moment as he realized his past had caught up with him. Even in this timeline. "Where are you?"

"Kristy and I are at the sheriff's office."

"Good. How am I supposed to contact him?"

"He gave me a phone number for you to call. He said you have four hours to call or they'll kill one of the kids to show they're serious, and that was two hours ago. You have to take their place, Alex. You have to save them!"

"I will, so just try to calm down. What's the phone number?"

Robert read the numbers to him. "Who are these people, Alex? What have you done?"

"It's a long story, Dad. Just stay where you are and I'll take care of it, all right?"

"You'd better. It's your fault your brother was murdered. So help me God, Alex, if any harm comes to my grandson, you'll regret it! Is that clear?"

Alex knew it was useless to explain what happened in Europe, so he didn't try. "I'll get them back. I promise."

He heard the phone being slammed down by his father and put his own phone away. He thought going back in time would give him a chance to mend their relationship, but he only managed to make things worse between them.

Okawna hadn't seen Alex so upset since he had lost Sevi. "What happened?"

"Boris Kinski has kidnapped my nephew."

Okawna slumped down in his chair. "I wondered if your past would come back to haunt you. Killing the members of the Russian Mafia was bad enough, but you should not have killed Boris's brother. You know how the Russians are when it comes to revenge."

Alex suddenly thought about Dieter's connection to Blacktooth in the other timeline and figured they would have been working together long before the incident on the island. "Would you mind asking Dieter to join us? I have a few questions for him."

Mike frowned. "I thought you said he was a murderer."

"He is. He's also a thief, but he has connections with the Russian Mafia, and right now, I need his help."

Mike grabbed the phone for the ship's intercom system. "John, please join me in my office."

***

Dieter was on the stern, talking to Harrison, when he heard the request from Mike. "Get Bartram and wait for me here. The only way off this ship is in the motorboat, so if it looks like I am in trouble, come to my rescue. Kill Okawna and his friend if you have to. Is that clear?"

Harrison was regretting getting involved with Dieter. He was hired to help steal the Mystic, not kill anyone, and if Dieter was in trouble, he did not want any part of it. He decided if it came down to a gunfight, Dieter was on his own. "Sure."

Dieter noticed the hesitation in Harrison's reply, and could only hope when the time came, he would do as ordered. He turned and went into the ship.

***

Okawna stared at Mike as he opened a desk drawer and gave him his revolver. He stood and tucked it into his pants at the small of his back, and remained standing when Dieter walked into the office.

Dieter could sense the tension of distrust in the air as he stepped inside and took a moment to study everyone's expressions. "You wanted to see me, Mike?"

"Not me. Mister Cave wants to talk to you."

Dieter wasn't sure how much they knew about his plan and decided to act unconcerned. "What can I do for you, professor?"

When Dieter called him professor, Alex realized some things had not changed, and hoped Dieter's connections were still the same, too. "Pull up a chair and sit down."

Dieter knew this wasn't just to chitchat and reluctantly did as asked. "What's this about?"

"I know you have connections in the Russian mafia, and I need you to locate someone for me."

Dieter tried to conceal his uneasiness by shifting his weight on the chair as he stared at Alex. "I do not know where you get your information, but I do not know anyone connected with the Russians."

Alex studied Dieter's expression before he dropped the hammer. "What about your friend, Blacktooth?"

The subtle change in Dieter's eyes told Alex he was right. Now he had to convince the captain it would be in his best interest to cooperate.

Dieter tried to remain impassive, wondering how this professor knew about Blacktooth. "You are asking the wrong person. I have never heard of him."

Alex reached into his jacket pocket and set an envelope on the desk. "This is a warrant from INTERPOL. They want you arrested for murder, and I've been authorized to take you into custody. I have one for Bartram, too."

Dieter shifted in his chair. "You must be mistaken, professor. I have murdered no one."

"Perhaps, but I'm sure Bartram will say you gave the orders. I'll make it simple. You help me, and I'll help you."

Dieter scoffed at the idea. "How could you possibly help me? You are just a college professor, so I do not think you are authorized to do anything to me."

"The Director of National Security is a good friend of mine."

Okawna grinned when he saw the change in Dieter's expression. He knew Alex would never ask Donner to let Dieter go free.

Dieter leaned forward. "Who are you trying to find?"

"Boris Kinski."

Dieter's eyes went wide. "He was the head of the Russian Mafia! Are you insane?"

Alex stared back evenly. "We have a history. Can you locate him or not?"

Dieter leaned back in his chair. "You are that Cave?"

"That's right."

"I have heard stories about you. They say you killed forty members of the Mafia, including Boris's brother. Tortured them first and then gave them a slow death."

Okawna looked down at Alex and laughed. "Forty? I thought it was only twenty."

Alex grinned. "Actually, it was six. Boris put his brother in charge of the operation to kill me, but the incompetent bastard made the mistake of killing my wife and leaving me alive. I have no regrets about what I did to him and his men."

Dieter grinned in self-satisfaction. He was right about Cave from the first moment he saw him climb out of the motorboat. He was a killer. "The last I heard, he was living in southeastern Siberia."

Alex shook his head no. "You'll have to do better than that if you want my help with INTERPOL. He has people here in the states right now, so I doubt he'll be too far away. After that fiasco with his brother, he'll want to keep a close eye on his people so they don't make the same mistake." He looked up at Okawna. "Give him the satellite phone."

Dieter realized he didn't have a way out of the situation unless he cooperated. "The phone numbers are programed into my cellphone. Take me to the mainland and I'll see what I can find out."

Alex leaned forward to stare into Dieter's eyes. "No deal. Where is your cell phone?"

Dieter felt a shiver run up his spine. "It's in my cabin, top left drawer."

Alex glanced up at Okawna, who left the room. He leaned back in his chair and grinned at Dieter. "Forty?"

Chapter 34

DARRINGTON, WASHINGTON:
When the van stopped, Derek and Jessica looked into each other's eyes, wondering if she would die. They waited anxiously as Mikhail climbed out and opened the side door, and then Jessica scrunched closer to Derek as they stared across a small field of grass to the tree line.

Mikhail smirked and pointed at Jessica. "Get over here."

Derek moved toward the door. "Take me instead."

"No. Just the girl."

When Derek didn't move, Mikhail pulled out his pistol. "Get back!"

Sasha climbed out of the van and walked around to the open door. "Stop playing with the girl and get them out."

Mikhail put away the pistol, brought out a set of wire cutters, and reached out toward Derek. "Give me your feet."

Once the zip tie was clipped free, Derek climbed out and turned to wait for Jessica. When Mikhail reached inside to cut her ankle strap, Derek used the distraction to slide a small knife from his front pocket, and then they followed Sasha around the van. When they saw a ranch-style house, Derek looked at Jessica and gave her a nod, knowing she was not going to be shot. At least, not yet.

*****

MYSTIC:
When Okawna returned to Mike's office, he held the cellphone out to Dieter while holding up the sat phone.

"Bring up the number on the screen and set it on the desk. I'll dial from this phone."

When Dieter did as asked, Okawna turned the speaker on and set the sat phone down. After four rings, it was answered.

"Who is this?"

Alex recognized Blacktooth's voice. When the captain leaned in toward the phone, he paid close attention to the tone in Dieter's conversation.

"It's Dieter. I need your help."

"What? You cannot change our deal."

"I need to find Boris. It's urgent."

"Are you crazy? What do you want that is so important?"

"He owes me money, and I need it to pay you."

"He has a safe house in the United States. It is a small town in Washington. Darrington, I think."

"Do you know the address?"

"One moment. Seven-eight-one Holly road."

"Thank you, my friend."

Alex looked at Mike. "Are we good here?"

"I'll take care of everything. Get him and his friends off my ship."

Okawna leaned away from the wall and looked at Mike. "I'll be back as soon as I can."

"We'll be fine, Okawna. Do what's necessary."

Everyone stood and left the office. When they arrived at the motorboat, Bartram was waiting for Dieter, but Harrison was nowhere to be seen.

Rita had been waiting in the lounge when she saw the four men headed out to the stern, and she crept out to the rear door and stared through the window. When she saw Alex putting handcuffs on Bartram, she realized her sense of paranoia was justified, but hadn't realized someone had walked up behind her.

"What's going on?"

Rita flinched and spun around, staring up at Joshua. "I don't know. I was just about to go find out."

Joshua reached over Rita's head and pushed open the door. "After you."

Mike noticed Rita and Joshua coming in their direction and waited until they joined the group. "Where is Harrison?"

Joshua indicated the inside of the ship. "When I woke up, he was sitting in his cabin."

Mike turned to Rita. "Go pack your belongings. Your service is no longer required." He looked up at Joshua. "Escort her down and bring Harrison back with you. Tell him he's fired, and I want him off my ship."

Rita felt a sense of relief. She realized this friend of Okawna must have powerful connections, so it was probably only a matter of time before they would learn what she was up to. She decided it was a good time to leave and followed Joshua back inside the ship and down to the cabins.

Dieter looked over at Alex when Okawna stepped behind him and slipped a Zip-tie around his hands. "I thought we had a deal?"

Alex smirked. "We do. I'll ask INTERPOL to wave the death penalty. I'm sure the word of a professor will make them change their minds."

Dieter glared at Alex. "You will not get away with this, Professor. I have connections all over the world. I will never see the inside of a prison, and I will hunt you down and make you suffer."

Okawna grabbed Dieter's arm in a vice-like grip. "Be careful stepping into the boat. I'd hate to see you fall overboard. I've heard people have a hard time swimming with their hands tied behind their back."

Okawna shoved Dieter toward the stern and did the same with Bartram, then followed them into the motorboat. Once

Rita and Harrison arrived and climbed in, Joshua joined them to bring the boat back when everyone was on the dock.

Alex held his hand out to Mike. "I appreciate your help, and I'll call you once my family is safe."

Alex climbed into the motorboat and Joshua took them to the dock below the Marina office. They left Rita and Harrison to fend for themselves, and put Dieter and Bartram in the back seat of the rental car. Alex waved at Mike, watching them from the bridge of the Mystic, and then climbed in and Okawna drove them out of the parking lot toward the Mount Vernon county jail.

Alex used his phone to call Donner. "I have them, Martin. Send the US Marshals to Mount Vernon to pick them up. Mike agreed to help salvage the device here in the Pacific, but a situation has developed, and Okawna's coming with me until it's resolved."

Donner listened while Alex explained what was happening to his family. "What can I do to help, Alex?"

"I won't know until Okawna and I check out the safe house. I'll call once I have a plan."

***

SPARROW VALLEY SHERIFF'S DEPARTMENT:
When Okawna drove the rental car into the parking lot, Alex recognized his father's old pickup truck. They parked in front of the station and climbed out, but Alex waited while Okawna looked around.

Okawna studied the old buildings. "So this is where you grew up. It reminds me of Stillwater."

"I thought the same about your hometown. I guess that's why we get along so well."

***

When Kristy heard the front door of the sheriff's office open, she looked up and smiled. "Uncle Alex!"

She leapt off the chair and ran up to him, and when he knelt down, she wrapped her arms around his neck. "Derek's been kidnapped, Uncle Alex."

"I know, and I'm here to rescue him."

Alex stood when his father walked into the room with a scowl on his face. "Hi, Dad."

"Get away from him, Kristy. It's his fault Derek's in trouble. Did you make the call?"

"Not yet."

"Damn it, Alex! You have less than an hour until that Boris person kills one of those kids!"

"I know, and we still have time to save them."

Robert looked at the blond-haired man. "Who are you?"

"My name is Okawna."

"He's my best friend, Dad. He's here to help."

Robert gave Okawna a brief appraisal and then looked at Alex. "We're running out of time."

Alex turned to Arnie. "Hello, Sheriff."

"Hi, Alex. I see you're still causing problems for your father."

Alex ignored the remark and turned to his dad. "I know where they are holding the kids. It's in Darrington, at seven-eight-one Holly Road."

Robert thought about it for a moment. "I know that house. It used to belong to the Dain family when I was a boy in Darrington."

"That's why I came here first. Okawna and I are going to check it out, and I need a description of the area around the house."

"That's not enough time to get there and back."

"We won't be coming back until we have the kids."

Robert stared at Alex. "I'm going with you."

"It's too dangerous. Okawna and I can handle it."

Robert ignored him and looked over at Okawna. "I have two deer rifles in my truck. Are you ready to go?"

Okawna looked at Alex, who indicated it was all right. "Yes, sir."

Robert looked down at Kristie. "Stay here with the sheriff until your cousin Jamie comes to pick you up." When he received a nod yes from her, he indicated for Okawna to lead the way and followed him out of the building.

Alex fumed as he turned and headed for the door. "Now I have to worry about him, too."

***

DARRINGTON:

Derek noticed Boris look at his watch and wondered what it meant. "You haven't told us why we're prisoners. I don't even know your names."

Boris glared at the boy, but didn't answer. Cave was running out of time. If he didn't call within the next ten minutes, the girl would be the first one he killed.

Derek looked over at the woman sitting in a stuffed chair. When Boris turned to talk to her, he opened his pocketknife and began cutting at the plastic strap around his wrist. He figured once the strap was cut, he could hang on to the long end to keep it around his wrist until it was the right time to fight back. The four men outside were armed, but he didn't see the man or the woman here inside carrying any guns.

Derek stifled a gasp when he cut his thumb and dropped the knife on the floor. He quickly used his shoe to shove it under the couch, silently cursing his clumsiness before the strap was cut.

***

THE WOODS BEHIND THE SAFE HOUSE.

Alex handed the small binoculars to Okawna. "I count two guards in the trees."

Okawna looked through the binoculars. "Same here. They're carrying machine guns with silencers, and it looks like Glock 9mm as side arms."

Alex crawled back into the forest to join his father, with Okawna right behind him. He looked at his watch and had five minutes until he had to make the call.

Robert stared up at his son. "What are you waiting for?"

Alex ignored him. "Okawna and I will take out the two guards in the trees. Once I get inside, wait for my signal. When you hear a single shot, the two guards outside will instinctively stop walking and run to the house. That's when you and Okawna take them out. And Dad, shoot to kill."

Alex brought out his cellphone and entered the number, and after two rings, Boris answered. "It's Alex Cave. I want my nephew and the girl back unharmed."

"You're cutting it close, Cave. Another minute and the girl would be dead."

"Just tell me where you want to make the exchange."

"Where are you?"

Alex had an idea to buy time. "I'm at the Mount Vernon Airport."

"I'm sure you know where Darrington is, so stop at the Mobil gas station and one of my men will pick you up. You have fifteen minutes or the girl dies."

"I need a couple of hours. I have to get a rental car first, and it's a long drive to Darrington."

"You have one hour."

"I'll be there."

Alex hung up and looked at Okawna. "There must be a fifth man inside. He's going to pick me up and bring me back here."

Okawna looked at his watch. "How much time?"

"Only an hour and I need to get to Mount Vernon and back. You'll have to deal with the guards in the trees."

"I'll take care of it. You'd better get going."

Alex looked at Robert. "Be careful, Dad."

"I can take care of myself. Just save Derek and the girl."

When Alex headed through the trees to the road and the rental car, Okawna studied Robert and his rifle. He just hoped the old man was capable of killing a person.

Chapter 35

DARRINGTON. WOODS BEHIND THE SAFE HOUSE:
Okawna put his hand on Robert's shoulder. "Keep still."
The two guards in the trees suddenly hurried across the large lawn. One talked on the radio as they entered the house.
Once they were out of sight, Okawna sat up. "Shit!"
Robert rolled over onto his hands and knees. "Now what do we do? Alex is walking into a trap!"
"If I know Boris, he won't kill Alex right away. He wants to make him suffer first."
Robert felt a sinking sensation in his stomach. "He'll make the kids watch, won't he?"
"I'm afraid so. I have an idea. After Alex gets here, drive your truck up to the house and act as if you are lost. That will distract the guards long enough for me to get up behind them, and I'll take them out one at a time."
"Are you crazy?"
Okawna grinned. "I suppose I am."
"Hey, look. A woman and one guard just drove away in a van."
Okawna managed to see the woman before the van drove away. "That's Sasha Kinski. I figured she'd be here."
"Who is she?"
"Bad news. Let's get to your truck and watch for the van to return."
Robert stood up. "Were you with Alex in the CIA?"
Okawna got up, and they headed for the truck. "Yeah, I'm the guy you should blame for your other son, not Alex."
"What do you mean?"

"It was my bullet that killed Boris's brother, Yeaman, that night. When the bullets flew, everything got crazy. Alex spun around and fired just as Yeaman was about to shoot him, but he missed, so I took him out. When Alex thought he'd finally killed Yeaman, I didn't have the heart to tell him otherwise. When we heard sirens, I got Alex out of Russia."

"Why was he acting that way?"

Okawna stared at Robert. "Didn't Alex tell you he was married?"

Robert suddenly stopped. "What? No, he never said a word."

"After Alex sliced off a piece of Boris's face, he got a little pissed and sent his thugs to kill him. They planted a bomb in Alex's place in Holland, but they didn't know Alex's wife was there, too. Alex was out getting flowers when it blew up, and then he went crazy until he killed Yeaman. Or thought he did."

Robert continued walking. "He never told me. After Ken was killed, I guess I never gave him the chance."

***

DARRINGTON:

When Alex drove into the Mobil station, the only other vehicle was a dark blue van. He parked beside it, but didn't get out and then the passenger window in the van went down and he recognized an old enemy. When he didn't open his door, she pointed a silenced pistol at him. "Hello, Sasha."

She smiled. "Handsome as ever, I see. Leave your gun in the car and get in."

"I'm not carrying."

Sasha looked over at the driver and indicated for him to get out, then turned back to Alex. "Climb out and take off your coat."

Alex opened his door and did as ordered while studying the man getting out of the van, and it was a guard from the trees. He figured Boris must have called them in after the phone call, and that meant Okawna had not had time to kill them.

After being frisked, Alex looked at Sasha and indicated his car. "I thought you'd be here, so I've brought a friend of yours."

Alex leaned into his car. "Get out and say hello to your old friend."

Dieter climbed out and stared at Alex. "What have you done? She's been trying to kill me!"

Sasha grinned. "Two for two, Alex? You really didn't have to be so nice to me. Both of you get in the van."

***

DARRINGTON. WOODS BEHIND THE SAFE HOUSE:

After the van drove past the turnoff, Okawna climbed out of Robert's truck and looked through the window at him. "Once you distract the guards, I'll come in from the trees. Be careful. If they act suspicious, leave. I'll try to take them out before it happens."

"Why don't you just take them out with the rifle?"

"I'm sure Boris will keep one guard inside, so Alex will be outnumbered. I need to be close to the house when the shooting starts, so I can get inside fast."

"All right. We're running out of time, so let's get it over with."

Okawna tapped his fist on the door. "Be careful."

When Okawna headed through the forest, Robert started his truck, but didn't move. He reached over to open the glove box and retrieved a 357 magnum revolver. He checked to make sure it had a full load, then set it on the seat beside him and put the transmission into drive.

* * *

THE SAFE HOUSE:

Sasha was first to stroll through the door and grinned at Boris sitting in a stuffed chair. "Cave brought us an added guest. Your friend and mine, that swindler from Sweden, John Dieter."

Dieter came in next and hurried over to Boris. "I can get you the money. Just give me a few days."

When Alex stepped through the doorway, he saw the way Dieter was begging for his life and was disgusted. He looked at the kids and Jessica looked frighten, but Derek had a look that said he was ready for anything.

When Mikhail from the van closed the door behind him, Alex turned to Boris. "So, how do you want this to play out?"

Boris sneered at him. "We all go for a ride and you get to watch me kill them."

Alex glanced over at Mikhail standing nearby, and Sasha standing behind the stuffed chair holding Boris. That makes one for Okawna to deal with outside.

When a gunshot came from outside, Alex drove his fist into Mikhail's face, sending him crashing over a table and he lost his gun. He swung around as Sasha brought her pistol up, ready to fire.

A curdling scream from Jessica distracted Sasha, so Alex twisted the pistol from her hand and drove his fist into her jaw as Mikhail got up from the floor, reaching for his pistol.

In one swift move, Alex brought Sasha's pistol around and fired. Mikhail soared backward through the air, and his gun dropped to the floor.

When Derek saw Boris staring at the gun, he gritted his teeth and forced his hands apart until the small cut he had made on the strap burst apart. When Boris noticed Derek was about to leap for the gun, he snatched it up first, swinging it up and aiming it at the boy.

"Cave! Stop or the boy dies!"

Alex didn't hesitate. Just aimed and fired.

Sasha watched Boris spin around and crumple to the floor. She opened a drawer in the end table, grabbed a pistol, and then swung it around toward Alex.

Okawna suddenly crashed through the front door, distracting Sasha, and Alex put his gun against her temple and fired. The back of her head was suddenly splattered against the wall, with the bloody brain matter slowly sliding down toward the floor.

Okawna swung his gun around, saw Dieter cowering in a corner, and had a strong urge to pull the trigger. "Get up and cut the girl loose."

Derek ran over to Alex and gave him a hug. "I knew you'd save us."

Robert came running through the doorway and saw Derek and Jessica alive and well. He released a long breath of relief until he saw Jessica appeared to be in shock. He moved the stranger, Dieter, out of the way and took her hand, and then eased her off the couch while shielding her eyes from seeing the wall as he guided her outside.

Derek looked around the room and at the bloody mess on the wall. "Now what happens?"

"We need to preserve the evidence, so we go outside and I'll call a friend of mine to clean up this mess."

***

Jessica was leaning against Robert's truck when she saw Alex come out onto the lawn. She stepped up to him and kissed him on the cheek. "Thanks for saving our lives, Mister Cave."

"You're welcome."

For some odd reason, Alex thought about Wesley's relationship with Jamie Parker in this timeline. "Do you know Wesley Patterson?"

"Sure, everybody knows Wesley. He married my sister, Jamie."

Alex smiled and looked over at his father. "Thanks for the help, Dad."

"Is it okay if we leave now?"

"Sure. Okawna and I will stay here until the police take over. I just have to make a call before the neighbors report hearing gunshots."

Robert grinned. "Don't you remember? Nobody around here cares about gunshots. People do a lot of hunting, and most of them have targets somewhere on their property."

"I'm sorry I got you into this, Dad. I never meant for any of this to happen. Just a mistake I made a long time ago."

Robert stared at Alex, seeing the strong resemblance to his older brother. Before today, he could not stand even looking at a picture of Alex, but now he knew it was time to be a family again. "I'm sure the kids are hungry after this ordeal. Would you have time to come over for dinner tonight?"

Alex stared at his father. "After all that has happened, you want to cook?"

Robert laughed. "Hell no. We'll go to the restaurant in Sparrow Valley. I'm sure my friend Wesley will join us, too. He's married to one of the Parker girls now. In my opinion, she seems a bit too young for him. She even made him cut his hair."

Alex grinned. "That would be great, Dad. Okawna and I will meet you there when we're through here."

Chapter 36

THE ISLAND:

Alex stared through the front window of the small military helicopter as it approached the inside of the crater. The last time he was here, things didn't end well, and he was afraid this new timeline might end up the same way. With Donner's help, the pilot was fully vetted for this top-secret project, and they had chatted for most of the trip from Adak.

He could see a Navy destroyer holding station one-hundred-yards from the island, with a helicopter gunship parked on its deck. He had decided it was only prudent to have support standing by if this timeline took a turn for the worse.

He looked back over his shoulder at Henry with his face pressed against the window. It took a little convincing to get him to agree to run the operation here on the island, and his only condition was David be the one to fly the ship.

He looked over at David, who wasn't the least bit nervous. He had made arrangements to have him flown to Adak, where he and Henry had picked him up. On the seat between them was a tan box with the hand device for getting inside the spacecraft, and a black box with four power crystals.

The pilot stared through the lower window as he slowly set down on the beach inside the crater and shut down the engine. Once everyone was out, Alex, Henry, and David walked over to the spaceship. After attaching a device to the side of the alien craft, a two-foot by six-foot high opening appeared.

After his friends stepped inside, Alex walked across the beach to the cave, but hesitated to enter. The device was where it should be, but if the sphere was in the cargo hold, it meant something didn't work out the way it was supposed to, and he might have to start all over. Yesterday had been the longest day he could ever imagine, and he could not remember the last time he had gotten any sleep.

He released a long sigh and entered the cave and then followed the side of the spacecraft down to the airlock. It was exactly the same as the last time, and he held his breath as he looked into the cargo hold. When the only thing inside was the fourth device. He laughed as he continued inside and saw the silver suit was missing, but stopped smiling when he thought about Fala. Would they still have that magnetic attraction for each other?

He climbed back out to the cave and headed back to the spaceship. When he stepped inside, he saw how excited his friends were over their new toy.

Henry hurried over when he noticed Alex walk in. "Oh, Alex. It is in perfect condition! David is just about to insert the new power crystals, so cross your fingers."

Alex was excited about having a working spaceship and watched David insert the first crystal. He expected something to happen, but then David frowned. Even after he inserted the fourth crystal, all the lights remained off. Alex thought perhaps in this future, it doesn't even work. He saw the disappointment in his friend's demeanor and realized this might take longer than expected, so he put his hand on Henry's shoulder. "I'm sure you and David can get it working, so I'll say goodbye."

David stepped down from between the chairs and walked over to Alex. "Not so fast. How do you know all this stuff?"

Alex understood Paladin's warning and felt bad he could not tell them what he had been through yesterday. "It's a long, long story, and maybe someday I can tell you, but for now, you'll just have to trust me. I'll see both of you later, and good luck."

Alex walked back out to the helicopter and climbed in as the pilot started the engine. A few moments later, they were headed back to Adak. He stared out the window and wondered what type of paradox he might have created by saving Laughing Wolf's life, and was looking forward to getting back home so he could unwind before driving to the Okawna Land and Cattle Company.

***

STILLWATER. ONE WEEK LATER:

When Alex drove into the parking area at the Okawna Ranch, he saw Fala sitting with Judith under the tree, and heard a high-pitched scream of joy as he stepped out of his SUV. He walked around to the opposite side to open the door for his passenger, and a moment later, Halona ran up to greet him.

"Are you the caveman?"

Alex smiled. "That's right. What's your name?"

"My name is Halona."

Alex helped Kristy out of the SUV. "Halona, this is my niece, Kristy Cave."

Halona smiled at Kristy. "Does that mean you're a cavegirl?"

They both giggled, and then Halona pointed toward the barn. "Do you want to see the horses?"

Alex smiled as he watched them walking toward the barn, talking and laughing together. *So far, so good,* he thought.

Okawna walked over to greet his friend. "Glad you could make it, Alex. I see you brought an icebreaker. Come on over and I'll introduce you to the rest of the family. My dad is still in bed recovering from the bypass surgery three days ago. The doctor said it was a good thing he got checked."

When they reached the tree, Fala and Judith got up off the lawn, and Okawna introduced them. Alex shook Judith's hand first, and fought hard to control his anxiety as he held out his hand to Fala, something he hadn't felt in a very long time. When she accepted, she had a curious look in her eyes.

"Have we met before, Alex?"

"Oh, I'm sure I would have remembered."

Fala smiled. "It's nice to meet you. Who's the girl? She and Halona seem to get along."

"That's my niece, Kristy. She came to stay with me for a couple of weeks."

"We should do something together with the girls."

"I'd like that."

The end.

I hope you enjoyed Red Energy, and I would appreciate it if you will take a moment to write a short review.

Thank you for your time.

James

Here is a preview of the next exciting Alex Cave Adventure.

GRAVITY

Chapter 1

BUFORD GLACIER, ICELAND:

A distant noise caused Baltistan Nilsson to look up from his equipment on the northern edge of the ice sheet. There had been a larger than normal amount of ice breaking away from the face, so he was taking readings on the rate of calving, using a small quad copter with a built-in video camera.

He knelt down to check the chopper when he heard a strange hissing noise. He stood and stared in the direction of the sound, but all he could see on the other side of an ice ridge was a large, vertical white cloud against the sky blue background.

He carried the copter up to the top of the ridge separating him from the steam plumes, where an ominous glow reflected sporadically from his sunglasses. As he pulled them off to get a better look, his eyes widened and his jaw sagged in disbelief.

"What in God's name is that?"

He realized no one would believe this without a video recording, so he quickly flipped the switch to power up the chopper. He stared at the screen and began recording and then turned the helicopter toward the steam cloud.

***

MONTANA STATE COLLEGE, BOZEMAN:

Alex Cave sat on the edge of his old wooden desk, gazing out over his second year geophysics students, all feverishly trying to finish final exams on the last day of class. The faces changed, yet the material remained much the same. Year after year, it was the same lectures, the same tests, and the same student performance.

He grimaced, wondering silently about his chosen profession at the college. He loved the subject, and teaching paid the bills, but even with the occasional field trip to interesting formations, the work was becoming all too boring. He felt like a caged animal required to perform the same trick repeatedly for a tiny bit of a reward.

Since the highly classified Red Energy Operation last year, he would do the occasional investigation of extraordinary circumstances for his friend, Martin Donner, who was the Director of National Security. However, occasional was the optimal word, and it wasn't enough to get him out of his monotonous rut.

He looked up at the clock and felt a sense of relief. In a few more minutes, his classes would end for the summer. When he heard a knock on the door, he turned to look and saw a man in a US Postal Service uniform standing on the other side.

He walked over to find out what he wanted. "Can I help you?"

The man held out an envelope. "Sorry to bother you, Professor Cave, but I need your signature."

Alex signed for the letter and read the return address as the man walked away. It was from Reykjavík, Iceland, with Urgent written in red letters.

The bell rang, and Alex looked at his students. "Have a great summer, everyone."

He stepped aside while they left his classroom and then sat at his desk to grab a letter opener. Inside the envelope were a round-trip airline ticket from New York to Iceland, and a single page note.

Hello Alex. I am Jeffery Sliven, the Director of the Nordic Volcanological Center, and I need your help with an unusual geological discovery. Director Martin Donner said this might interest you. Below you will find the time, date, and location of the symposium we will hold with other top professionals in your field. I know this is short notice, but your expertise would be greatly appreciated.

Sincerely, Jeffery.

Alex felt a small adrenalin rush, thinking about the potential for a new challenge. He called the local airport and got a connecting flight to New York, but it would leave in two hours. As exhilarated as he was at the prospect of a new adventure, Alex knew his girlfriend, Fala, would not be happy about his having to leave again.

He tucked the envelope into his briefcase and headed out the door. When he reached the parking lot, he climbed into his SUV and headed home.

***

Alex drove into the driveway on his small ranch and parked next to his girlfriend's SUV. When he climbed out, he heard a familiar giggle and smiled. Halona, Fala's nine-year-old daughter, was playing tug-of-war with his dog, Barney, a mixed-breed he had rescued from an animal shelter as a pup, who had grown up to look more like a brown bear than a dog.

When Alex knelt down, Barney let go of the thick rope to run to him, causing Halona to fall on her butt. She laughed and jumped up, running after the dog.

When they both stopped in front of him, Alex ran his hand through Barney's thick fur. "How you doing, big fella?"

Halona smiled and held the rope out for her friend to see. "I won, Alex."

Alex grinned, swept her up onto his arm, and stood up. "I saw that. You're getting stronger every day. Has your mom been giving you some kind of magic Native American growing medicine?"

Halona laughed. "No, silly. I'm just growing tall, like her."

"You sure are, so it's time you do your own walking."

He set her on the grass. "See if you can beat Barney again, while I go talk to your mom."

Halona looked up at Alex and frowned. "You're leaving again, aren't you?"

Alex knelt down in front of her. "I'm afraid so."

"Will you be back for my birthday party on Sunday?"

Alex loved Halona as much as he loved her mother, who had planned the party several weeks ago, and he dare not miss it. "I promise I'll do my best to be here."

Her lower lip fell into a pout. "All right."

Alex stood and climbed the steps onto the back porch. When he looked back, Halona and Barney were playing again, so he went into the house.

***

Alex set his briefcase near the hallway and found Fala sitting in a chair in the living room. Because of her raven black hair, her parents had given her the Native American word for crow.

Fala looked up from her laptop when she heard the door open, saw Alex, and smiled. "Somebody sure looks excited. I bet you're happy to be done with classes for the semester."

"Definitely, but that's not why I'm excited. I've been asked to attend an urgent geological meeting in Iceland."

Fala's smile was immediately replaced with a scowl. Nearly slamming her laptop on the coffee table, she stood. "Iceland? Are you kidding me, Alex?"

"What?"

"You just got out for the summer and I thought we might finally do some traveling together. All three of us, or maybe you and I could go somewhere. Between classes and your mysterious rock excursions, I feel like we don't see you enough. Hell, I don't see you enough."

Alex walked over, grabbing her around the waist and pulling her close to him. "Fala, you know I love you."

Fala smirked slightly and rolled her eyes, "You have a funny way of showing it, traveling around the world, leaving me here to feed your dog and bring in your mail."

"How about this? When I get back, we'll make time for us. We'll take Halona to your parents, then we'll go on a little trip. Just the two of us."

"You promise?"

He kissed her on the lips. "Of course."

"Why wait, Alex? There are thousands of perfectly qualified geologists in the world that can handle a little rock crisis in Iceland. Let one of them deal with it."

"I can't. Not this time. I have to go."

Fala pulled out of his grasp. "No, Alex. You want to go. There's a big difference."

Alex stared after her as she stormed into the kitchen to start dinner. He knew she was right, but he still wanted to go to Iceland. Something about the urgency of the message gnawed at him.

Fala slammed cupboard doors and tossed silverware into drawers. "Will you be joining us for dinner, or will you be leaving right away?"

Alex stood in the kitchen doorway, watching her slam the oven door closed and toss a pot of water on the stove to boil. "My flight leaves in less than an hour, so I'll leave as soon as I finish packing."

Fala stopped in her tracks, folded her arms across her chest, and stared at Alex. "Well, when do you plan on being back? You know Halona's birthday party is on Sunday. She'll be crushed if you're not here."

"I know, and I promise I'll try to be back on time."

"Don't make promises you don't intend to keep, Alex. The last time you went off on one of your geological symposiums or digs or whatever it is you keep running off to do, you said the exact same thing. You know, my parents went to a lot of trouble arranging the ceremony with the Cherokee leaders to welcome you into our tribe."

"I know, and I apologized to them, but this time it's different. They just need my opinion about a geology problem."

Fala uncrossed her arms and went back to fixing dinner. As she searched through the cupboards, slamming the doors as she went, she shook her head, "Yeah, right. The last time you came back from one of your 'geology' trips, your face was all bruised and you had three broken ribs. Since when did studying rocks become so dangerous?"

Alex stepped into the kitchen and smiled as he grabbed Fala's hands. "I'll be in an auditorium on a university campus this time."

He felt Fala's hands relax slightly in his and looked into her dark brown eyes. "Are we okay?"

When Fala nodded hesitantly, he kissed her on the cheek and walked down the hallway to his office to grab a suitcase from the closet and his passport from the desk drawer. He continued to the master bedroom and packed for a short trip. When he entered the bathroom, he opened the only drawer out of six that was his, and grabbed his shaving bag, and then went back and added it into his suitcase.

He returned to the living room, where Fala was in the kitchen. "I'm all set."

Fala moved to the kitchen doorway, her disposition having softened considerably since he had packed. "Do you need a ride?"

"No thanks. Actually, I don't think I'll be gone more than one night, and I'm not sure what time I'll be getting back. I'll take my truck so you don't have to leave your veterinary clinic to pick me up."

"All right. Just call me when you get back."

"I will."

When he turned and headed for the back door, Fala followed him out outside. She just hoped he was telling the truth about staying in an auditorium.

***

Fala followed Alex to his car and waited while he said goodbye to Halona and then wrapped her arms around his neck. "Be careful, Alex."

He kissed her lips. "I will. I'll call when I'm headed back."

When Alex drove away, Fala climbed the steps up to the deck and sat in a chair. She knew about Alex's past of working for the CIA, and he had promised never to work for them again, but for the last four months, she suspected on some of his supposed field trips he was really doing some kind of secret mission for the Director of National Security. Whatever he was doing on those occasions, it sure wasn't studying rock formations.

She wanted a comfortable family life, with a husband who doted on her, a father who adored her daughter, and family dinners together every night. She wanted a chance to travel across the country on summer vacation like a normal family, not stuck here alone for weeks at a time while Alex ran off on some adventure.

This new trip to Iceland didn't sit well with her. She had a bad feeling this excursion was some type of secret mission, and Alex would wind up getting hurt again, or worse, killed.

Fala looked away from the pasture when she felt a small hand on her shoulder and turned to see her daughter's troubled expression. "What's on your mind, sweetie?"

"You looked sad, Mom, so I came over to cheer you up."

Fala smiled. "Well, thank you, baby. You did. Shall we have some supper?"

"Is Alex going to get hurt again?"

Fala's smile slipped away. She realized she wasn't the only one worried about Alex's safety on this new trip. "We'll ask the Spirits to watch over him after we eat, okay?"

"All right."

Award-winning author James M. Corkill is a Veteran, and retired Federal Firefighter from Washington State, USA. He was an electronic technician and studied mechanical engineering in his spare time before eventually becoming a firefighter for 32-years and retiring. He has since settled into the Smokey Mountains of western North Carolina and has a fantastic view from his writing desk.

He began writing in 1997, and was fortunate to meet a famous horror writer named Hugh B. Cave, who became his mentor. In 2002, he rushed to self-published a dozen copies of Dead Energy so his wife could see his book published before she was taken by cancer. When his soul mate was gone, he stopped writing and began drinking heavily.

His favorite quote. "When you wake up in the morning, you never know where the day will take you."

In 2013, he met a stranger who recognized his name and had enjoyed an old copy of Dead Energy, except for the ending. When she encouraged him to start writing again, he realized this chance meeting was just what he needed to hear at the right moment. He quit drinking and began the rewrite of Dead Energy into The Alex Cave Series, and thankful for that fateful encounter.

Other books by James M. Corkill
Dead Energy. The Alex Cave Series Book 1.
Cold Energy. The Alex Cave Series Book 2.
Gravity. The Alex Cave Series Book 4.
Pandora's Eyes. The Alex Cave Series Book 5.
DNA. The Alex Cave Series Book 6.
Parallel. The Alex Cave Series Book 7.
Impact Yellowstone

Movie scripts available from the author.
You can contact him at. Jamesmcorkill@gmail.com

www.ingramcontent.com/pod-product-compliance
Lightning Source LLC
Chambersburg PA
CBHW070501120726

47910CB00003B/1084